MW01673694

Jon Bragg Scout's Honor

Jon Bragg, Volume 2

Kenney Myers

Published by Kenney Myers, 2021.

This is a work of fiction. Similarities to real people, places, or events are entirely coincidental.

JON BRAGG SCOUT'S HONOR

First edition. October 14, 2021.

ISBN: 978-1736571132

Written by Kenney Myers.

Table of Contents

To my wife Jolene & our children Ashley, Kelsey, & Joseph.

May every day be an adventure and may you know how much you are loved and cherished by me!

To my parents, Rick & Gracie

Thank you for your support and love through the years. I am so blessed to call you Dad and Mom!

Nightmare

Jon

"I HAVE BEEN HAVING this nightmare off and on for months now," Jon says, shaking his head in disbelief. "I am in a dark, dreary place, and someone I care about is being tortured by someone I cannot make out who it is. But I desperately want to help them and can't, completely unable to move. I can't speak, I can't move, and I'm just paralyzed with fear as I watch through barely open eyes."

Grandpa just looks back at me with his hand on his chin, stroking his long, gray beard, as if it will somehow provide him with an answer as to why this is happening to me. He starts to speak several times then pauses, shaking his own head, obviously not sure of the right answer. He then says, "Jon, it's normal to have dreams that put us in situations where we want to use our powers, but for some reason can't. I highly doubt you have anything to worry about; it's just a dream. Why don't we take a break from Bragi training today so you can go and enjoy a nice summer day with Marc? Maybe go to the park, or play that video game you love, or whatever you kids are interested in this week. I can't keep up."

I smile and think to myself, *I could use a break*, but I just say, "Thank you, Grandpa!"

As I get changed, I reflect on all that has happened since I learned I was a descendant of Bragi, Odin's second eldest son, which makes me an Asgardian who inherited some of his power. What's interesting is that, ever since I was a kid, I enjoyed reading about Loki and Thor, all the way up to Ragnarök.

Ragnarök is the epic battle between the gods that represented law and order, and the giants that represented chaos that were led by Loki. Almost the entire universe was destroyed and, while I knew that some Asgardians survived, I didn't imagine that there could be half-human offspring, let alone that my family line contained them.

Bragi is the god of poetry and was able to use words and the fine arts to manipulate humans, all animals, and influence the basic elements. This is in addition to the usual powers that all Asgardians enjoyed of strength, healing, and overall durability.

However, descendants like me never really know what powers they might inherit. It varies quite a bit, but it would be rare for all of the powers to be triggered. For me, I have always loved reading and writing poetry in my journal. It turns out that, being Bragi, those rhymes that I used to write for fun suddenly became powerful and allowed me to do things that I never dreamed was possible, as long as I follow a few basic rules.

This past winter, I also learned about the descendants of Loki who were stripped of their powers by the Asgardian Protection Society (APS) for violating the rules against abusing their abilities for personal gain and revealing us to humans in the process. They were warned for centuries but couldn't resist the temptations. Eventually, the sentence was carried out to end their line a few generations ago. However, being Loki, they were tricksters who figured out how to drain the blue essence—our source of power—from other Asgardians to temporarily restore their abilities. The only problem is the Loki's line needed a steady supply of blue essence to keep it going, which led them to start hunting down Asgardians, like my grandpa. They killed Grandma, stripped Grandpa of his blue essence, and left him in a catatonic state. He was left mumbling a rhyme over and over, and it turns out that Grandpa was pretty darn smart, as well, because he was waiting for me to come into my powers so I would repeat that rhyme and free his mind, which actually worked!

You see, when someone from an Asgardian line turns sixteen, they either ascend to their power or they do not, and it skips that generation. Well, this Loki knew that newly ascended Asgardians had the most blue essence and, accordingly, he became a high school gym teacher and wrestling coach to make it easier for him to find new ascendants. Surprisingly, this Loki, known to us in Grinwell as Coach Locke, had a son, Dustin, who also inherited the gift of Loki. This is notable as it usually skips a generation, or even two. The working theory that the APS has is that it has to do with their use and manipulation of blue essence.

Coach Locke ended up here in Grinwell, Iowa after he found some items at Grandpa's house that led him here. Grandpa had legally changed his last name so Coach Locke didn't know which of the students at Grinwell High School might be related to him, so he and Dustin started testing students using various ways, and it really got out of hand. In the end, they mistook my best friend, Marc, for a descendant of Thor, and that's when I came to his rescue.

With the help of Grandpa, we were able to destroy the Lockes and their blue essence extraction equipment. However, ever since then, I have been having those nightmares. I just cannot shake them, and I am also having trouble forgiving myself for ending them, even if they were as evil as can be. It's just a lot to deal with, and I guess maybe that is why I keep having these dreams out of guilt, thinking I deserve to be punished.

As I step outside, I realize Grandpa was right; this is a perfect Iowa summer day. The sun is shining brightly, it's a warm eighty degrees, but there is no humidity. It feels fantastic as the sun warms my face, followed by a nice, cool breeze that is just short of sending a slight chill through my body. It's the perfect balance of warmth from the sun and coolness in the shade. I love Iowa weather this time of the year.

I hop into my sensible sixteenth birthday gift—my used Toyota Corolla—and drive over to Marc's house.

As Marc steps out of his house, I realize he has changed, as well, since this all started.

Marc and I have always been kind of slight in stature, but now we have both grown a couple of inches and have filled out considerably. Since I came into my power, I have gotten quite a bit stronger so, while I haven't had a huge need to work out, Marc has taken to going to the gym so he can "be a better sidekick." It's a CrossFit gym, so the workouts are super intense, but boy have they made a difference in his overall fitness level.

The first time Marc went, he thought he was going to pass out from the intensity, but now he is at the front of the pack for every set of drills. I know he means well, but with my powers, I'm not super likely to need his assistance when, and if, a threat arises. I know that's not really at the heart of why he is working out so hard. I'm sure he partially just wants to keep up with me, and I'm more than happy to support him. I want him to feel good about himself, because he is a great person and has a ton to offer the world, whether he has Asgardian powers or not.

His power is his mind and the ability to always think about how different scenarios might play out. He's a perceptive guy, and I'm sure that will come in handy some day for both of us. Even if it doesn't, that's totally fine. I am just lucky to have such a good best friend.

Geesh, okay, I need to pull it together. It's time for some summer fun, and Marc is all smiles as he walks up to the car.

"Hey, how's my favorite Asgardian today?" Marc says as he gets into my car.

I immediately give him the look that says, "*Really? You know better; we don't talk about this out in the open.*" Then I look in both directions then back at Marc.

He continues looking at me like he expects an answer, so I relent.

"Fine, Marc, how's my trusty sidekick?"

This brings a huge smile to his face as he buckles up. "Feeling great and ready to take on the world. Let's go!"

This has become our little routine and, while it may seem silly, there's comfort in knowing how our day is always going to start. If it didn't start this way, at this point, it would be kind of weird. So, we are off to cruise the streets of Grinwell, looking for something to do, someone to save, or just listening to "Old Town Road" and singing along with our windows rolled down. It's summer, and we just can't help ourselves.

Blue Hill

Darla

AS I LOOK AROUND MY room, it reminds me that I want more and that I expect more, for and from myself. I see several dance and track ribbons, medals, and whatnot, but most of those are from my old dance company and school in West Des Moines.

My parents moved me here, to Blue Hill, during this past school year, which isn't easy for a sophomore in high school, but they didn't have much of a choice, and I understand that. My grandpa passed away, and my grandma didn't have the strength to run the family farm, so my dad left his engineering job to come back to Blue Hill and take over the farm.

Grandma died shortly after Grandpa, so now it's just us. It's been interesting since he hasn't worked on the farm in decades, but he has a big heart and is figuring it out as he goes. We are well into the summer now, and the crops are doing fine, so I guess that's a good thing. I don't mind the chores at all. I have always enjoyed working hard, and I like waking up early, so that part has been fun. Plus, I get to spend time with my dad in the morning, and I hardly saw him when he worked at his old job. Although, a small part of me does wish we could just go back to West Des Moines so I can finish out high school and continue with my dance team there. For now, though, I need to focus on the upcoming dance competitions for my new team from Grinwell.

Grinwell is about ten miles from Blue Hill, but it's large enough to have a dance studio, thank goodness. It's not quite the same as my old company, but we are on our way to Nationals, nonetheless. I guess

I better get used to Grinwell, because our high school in Blue Hill announced that we will be merging with them in the fall. So, that will be the third high school for me, and yet one more time where I have to go through the awkward new kid in school that isn't quite like everyone else thing.

At some point, the Grinwell girls will ask, and I will say that my parents met in college at Drake University and, according to them, "fell in love at first sight." It's not that I ask, but for some reason, Mother and Dad feel the need to remind me, usually when they are snuggling on our ancient, lime-green sofa. Gross and gross. Then I will explain that my mother is from Costa Rica originally and comes from a culture that is matriarchal, called the BriBri. She is also quite dark-skinned, and I inherited a lot from her in both looks and strength.

I am one of those girls who never backs down from a challenge and certainly not a challenge from any boy. It's not that I am a tomboy—not that I would mind the term—I am just the type of person who always gives one hundred percent and never backs down. To me, that is just normal and who I am. It gets me into some trouble every now and then, but I wouldn't have it any other way. I am proud of who I am, and ready and willing to stretch the limits of my abilities whenever possible. In fact, I am doing that more and more lately, and I am far from finished. Let's just say the boys from Grinwell better get ready to be challenged, too. Speaking of which, I better get around to going to practice.

I don't have too long before ...

Clap! Clap! Clap!

Ugh ... too late.

Followed by Mother yelling, "Darla! Let's go!"

For whatever reason, Mother claps to get my attention when I am up in my room, and it is one of those noises that pierces your soul and immediately elicits a negative but effective reaction. I don't think I could dislike a noise more than that one.

I call back down, "I'm coming, Mother." Then I start running around the room, gathering everything that I need to jam into my bag. I need my two dance costumes, and then ... *Where are my ballet shoes?*

"Mother, where are my ballet shoes?"

She answers, "In the car, remember?"

Whew. Okay.

I run into the bathroom and take a quick look. Yep, still me.

My hair is a bit long right now. It's pretty much pitch-black. I am going to pull it back into a ponytail as quickly as humanly possible, a highly acquired skill that has taken years of practice but comes in handy, to say the least.

I'm not a makeup person, thankfully, so I don't have to waste time with that. I don't have a problem with girls who wear makeup; I just don't feel the desire to use it myself, especially not for a sweaty dance practice. Of course, for the dance competitions, that is all taken care of by the moms backstage, but this is just a practice, so moving right along.

I take a quick look to size myself up and make sure everything is in order. Then I hop on the scale real quick, knowing Miss Sally, our dance instructor, is going to make us do that today before practice. Okay, I am good. Right at one twenty-two, which puts me solidly in the "normal range," as Miss Sally puts it, for my body mass index. I'm not sure why she focuses on details like that. As long as we can dance, that's all that matters, right? In any event, I just check to avoid being hassled.

As soon as I get downstairs, I see Mother standing by the door with her arms folded, as if she has been waiting a million years.

"Dance practice is the same time every day, Darla. Why do you insist on always risking being late?"

I know better than to respond with what I am really thinking. Been there, done that. So, I just shrug and make my way over to the door, which is already open by the time I get there with Mother already several steps ahead of me. Then it's down the porch stairs and heading to the driveway.

I quietly make my way to the car and drop my bag in the back seat. I have my driver's license, but I head over to the passenger's side because, with Mother, it's just better if she drives. Driving with her is like a nonstop lesson and pop quiz with every decision you make being scrutinized, as if deep thought went into it. *Why did you adjust the mirror? Why did you slow down too soon/too late? Are you going to leave that turn signal on the whole trip?* Yeah, it's just not worth it. Dad, on the other hand, barely says a word and just goes along for the ride. Hopefully, he picks me up so I can drive home. He's usually done in the fields by then.

Mr. Whiskers

Jon

MARC AND I QUICKLY get tired of listening to Billy Ray Cyrus and move on to a discussion of the training sessions that I have had so far, which has been numerous. We have learned that I do have the ability to manipulate most living things, including plants, animals and, of course, people. I also have the ability to control electronic devices, mechanical devices, and even some more basic objects, like clothes, paper, and other small household items. I have at least some ability in manipulating the elements—earth, wind, fire, and water. However, we haven't fully explored all of those since they require some complexity in the rhymes and have significantly riskier effects.

As Grandpa describes it, the main risk that I must worry about is the threat of my powers being exposed to humans. Manipulating elements is generally hard to explain if someone witnesses it. If a paper moves, or some other such item, it's easy to explain it away as a breeze or draft. If it randomly combusts ... that might be a bit harder to explain.

As is usually the case with any conversation that Marc and I have surrounding my gifts, eventually, we gravitate toward an experiment, and I have something in mind.

Whoa! I swerve to miss an animal in the road.

Being from Grinwell, it's pretty common to have various animals accidentally getting run over, also known as roadkill, which is a particularly disturbing yet accurate term.

I decide to stop the car to check on it, which also gives me an idea on something new to show Marc, depending on what we find.

As we get closer to the animal, my heart sinks a little. I can see it was a cat, and not a stray. It was a Maine Coon with a dapper black coat and white chest, wearing a red collar with a black tag on it to identify its owner. We check the tag, finding he belonged to Mr. Lemke, a retired teacher from Grinwell High. That's not surprising since we have all lost count of how many cats he has at his small house on the outskirts of town.

It's sad to see this cat lying there. I'm sure Mr. Lemke will be devastated when he finds out.

Mr. Whiskers, the cat, has a peaceful look in his eyes that are calling to me, which is the something new I want to show Marc.

I whisper to the cat, "As I peer into your blue eyes, give me a vision of what caused your demise. Just a glimpse is all I will take, so I will know what caused this awful mistake."

Just then, I see a vision of a big, brown dog chasing Mr. Whiskers. He was running across the road when a red sports car with the plates "*IBEQB1*" hit him. At least it was a quick death for this furry fellow.

As I explain everything to Marc, we carefully gather Mr. Whiskers up to take to Mr. Lemke so he could give him a proper burial.

When we arrive at Mr. Lemke's house, to my surprise, I see the same red Camaro—of course we all know it belongs to Brad Dillon, the starting quarterback for the Grinwell High football team, who looks exactly like Captain America meets Ken doll. He's consoling Mr. Lemke, which means he already told him what happened. Immediately, my respect for Brad goes up several notches, from the guy who is dating the girl who I have had a crush on since forever to an okay guy, I guess.

We carefully grab Mr. Whiskers and bring him over to where Brad and Mr. Lemke are standing. Mr. Lemke looks over at us with a nod of greeting then picks up Mr. Whiskers from my arms. For an older guy with skin as tough as leather and gray hair flowing in the wind, he holds that cat like a baby, just engulfing him in his arms. He clearly loved Mr.

Whiskers. I don't think any of us has dry eyes at this point, so touched by this show of pure love.

Mr. Lemke then shakes our hands and asks us to leave him be, which we honor, of course.

Brad, Marc, and I all walk back to our cars and silently get into them. I give a nod over to Brad, and he returns it as we both drive off, heading in separate directions. It's so quiet that all you can hear is the engine and AC churning, rattling, and blowing. It goes on like this for a few minutes as we gather our thoughts.

After a little while, Marc looks over and says, "Are we going to talk about what just happened? That was pretty amazing. You saw exactly how Mr. Whiskers died and even described Brad's car and his license plate! How long have you known you could do that? What was it like?"

I shrug. "It's something Grandpa and I have been working on recently, but with smaller animals. I can't see everything in their minds, but I do get a glimpse of what caused their deaths. It's a strange and disturbing feeling, but also an important skill to develop. Grandpa has no doubt that, at some point, the APS will come looking for me for my ability to do what you just saw. For now, let's treat it like another trade secret that only we know."

Marc nods in understanding. He's not done just yet, though, and that does not surprise me even a little bit.

"Can you imagine how many murders you could help the police solve?"

"Yes, but if I were to do that, then they would for sure know that there is something different about me, and that could risk everything. I took an oath and registered with the APS. I have to be careful to not expose us."

Marc slumps down in his seat a little but nods, knowing I am right.

After the Loki incident, Grandpa called the APS. He confirmed that they indeed came, cleaned up and disposed the blue essence extraction equipment, or anything that was left of it, along with the

Loki line. Grandpa had to describe what happened to him, and that forced him to reveal that I was also a Bragi. This led to several discussions with the APS over the last couple of months as they questioned me and put me through their new member training program.

Essentially, every new Asgardian descendant has to register with them then learn a really long list of do's and don'ts that we are bound to abide by. I'm not really sure what the *or else* scenario is there, but it's really not a problem for me. I understand the rules and appreciate them for what they are, which is a way to keep our secret safe and to respect the gifts that we have been given from our ancestors.

We are assigned a mentor. In my case, it was Grandpa, which is perfect since Grandpa still lives with us, and we have all of his Bragi books and notes in our garage. We set up a magic training area in our basement and really built that level out to be an apartment for him, so he has some privacy when he and I both need it.

At the end of the APS training program, each trainee is required to take an oath. This oath is sacred and binds us in different ways to curtail some of the uses of our powers to specifically limit our ability to manipulate things for our own personal gain. This especially focuses on wealth and matters of the heart, so we cannot use our powers to conjure up millions of dollars or to make someone fall in love with us. The most important pledge is to do no harm to humans and to keep our secret to the grave, which we swear to on our honor, our Asgardian honor. This is something Marc knows I take seriously. We have been in the Boy Scouts for years, and he knows how seriously I take my Scout's Honor, so he doesn't question me on principle. Plus, what is more epic than a sacred oath?

Dancing with Jess

Darla

WHEN WE PULL INTO THE parking lot of the dance studio, the team is still lined up outside, just hanging out. That means the classes before us have gone longer, as usual, which is fine. It gives us time to catch up.

Mother stops well before we get to the front so she can avoid dodging dancers and drive back out the way she came.

As I get out of the car, she says, "Don't dilly dally when it is time to go tonight. Dad will be picking you up, and he will be tired after working all day, so don't make him wait."

I nod and say, "Sure thing, Mother. Bye."

As she pulls out, I think, *If Dad is going to be so tired, maybe you should come and pick me up*, but that is a fight I do not want to pick with her at this time. Plus, I really do want Dad to pick me up. I also know full and well that, if Dad is waiting, he is more than happy to catch a quick nap in the car, so I have nothing at all to worry about.

As I start to walk over, someone jumps on my back and puts their arms around my neck.

I just say, "Get off me, Jess!"

"How did you know it was me?"

I shake my head. "Because it is always you."

Jess Friggens is a super popular girl from Grinwell, a cheerleader and dating the captain of the football team. All-in-all, a really good person to know and, on top of that, we are doing a duet together for Nationals. As soon as she found out that Blue Hill and Grinwell would be combining schools, she was beyond excited and immediately went to work recruiting me for cheer and telling me nonstop how much fun we're going to have this coming year. I'm not so sure about that.

One thing that was nice about Blue Hill was that it was so small you could pretty much do anything that you decided you wanted to do. They always needed more people for every extracurricular activity from theater, to band, cheer, and literally every sport. It was kind of fun and nice to know that you could literally try anything that you wanted to try, as long as you asked and gave it a good effort. Even if you didn't give a good effort, it almost had to be better than not having anyone do it. The combined school will result in more competition for virtually everything. I guess that's fine. I certainly never back down from a good challenge. Yet, it is decidedly more limiting in many ways.

I know Grinwell High School has had its share of issues lately, at least from a teacher perspective. They lost not one but two wrestling coaches last year. One was attacked by a bear or something and the other just up and left, and nobody has heard from him since. That coach also had a son who was a state wrestling champion, and he hasn't surfaced anywhere, either. At least not in Iowa. I wonder where he is. He was so good.

As I'm about to ask Jess some more questions about that, the front door swings open and Miss Sally tells us to line up. She is a prototypical dancer who still shows us quite frequently the "correct" way to do all the moves. It's really quite impressive. After all, she must be in her forties by now. She always has her brown hair with blonde highlights pulled up into a nice, tight bun on the top of her head and is always wearing dance clothes, usually with tights and dance shoes that are appropriate for the style of the day.

She clears her throat several times as we all line up. "As you go into the studio, be sure to stop by the scale to be weighed by Miss Julie. If any of you would like to get weighed after the workout today, as well, that is fine. We need everyone to be on their best behavior and in good shape for the warm-up dance competition this weekend."

We all take our turns entering and going through the normal routine. Step on the scale, write down your weight, get an unsolicited tip for weight loss, eye roll, and off into the dance room.

Today is contemporary dance, and it begins like normal with our warm-ups. This includes jumping jacks, running in place, neck stretches, and various other completely normal exercises that you would do to get ready for any sport. We then begin working on our routine for the competition, which is quite involved, but we all know it so well by now that we move as one unit and everything seems to be going fine.

Miss Sally steps in, watching the class with her arms folded, then pacing around the room, looking each of us up and down then shaking her head in disapproval. This is completely normal, and we all know what is going to come after the music stops.

Miss Sally says, "Girls, girls, girls that is just not going to be good enough. Kristen, you are off by half a beat into the first turn every time. Eva don't even get me started with your lack of extension in general. Let's take it from the top and try to put together at least one solid run today."

We all look at each other and nod, knowing we can do this.

Despite what Miss Sally says, we really aren't that far off. We just have to focus and all of these smaller problems will shake out.

We dance again, and again, and again with no breaks and with similar feedback from Miss Sally. It's starting to take its toll on all of, us and we are getting tired.

Class is about over and, by the look on all our faces, you can tell. The last dance was probably the worse one we did.

When it's over, Miss Sally claps three times, which is high praise, and then says, "Duets and solos meet me in dance room B across the hall."

Oh brother, we aren't done yet.

I turn to Jess. "Are we supposed to practice our duet today?"

"No," Jess responds, "that's tomorrow, but I guess we are about to find out."

We both shrug then force our exhausted bodies to move forward and over to the next dance room. And, as we enter, we see that Miss Sally is talking with Jill, who is slightly younger than us and is competing as a soloist at the junior competition level.

"Girls," Miss Sally says, "I want you to watch Jill and try to learn from her. Watch her extension, watch the fluidity in which she moves and, most importantly, the emotion that you feel when you watch her dance. Dancing is like storytelling—each step and movement should invoke emotion. Sit, watch, learn."

The music starts up, and we are immediately hit with a fresh wave of excitement, anticipation, and a little bit of nervousness for Jill. Hopefully, she does well. This is a lot of pressure for Miss Sally to throw onto her.

It's also a little insulting, too. I mean we are at the senior competition level. Then again, we are quickly and completely in awe of what we are seeing Jill do.

Wow, her routine is awesome!

Picking Up Jill

Jon

WE RESUMED DRIVING around town a bit and just started to talk about what we wanted to do with the rest of the night. Should we head back for some gaming action or maybe catch a movie? Our little theater here in Grinwell only shows slightly older movies, though, and ... well, we have already seen everything that is showing, so that's out.

As we head back to my house, Mom calls.

"Hey, Jon-boy, can you head over to dance and pick up Jill? Dad and I are running behind, and her class should be over in a few minutes."

Normally, I wouldn't be too excited about this chore, but we have already exhausted all our ideas, so I quickly say, "Sure, Mom, that works! We will see you in a bit."

Mom already knows Marc is in the car, so she says, "Thank you. See you boys later."

With that, we are off on a mission. Not a super exciting one, but "beggars can't be choosers," as Dad always says.

We make our way over to the dance studio, and I notice that Jess's car is in the parking lot. I point it out to Marc and say, "Let's go in and say hi to Jess, too."

Jess and Jill aren't on the same dance team. Jill is on the younger team, but boy, was she upset when she didn't get asked to join the senior team last fall. I can understand. She has been working really hard, and everyone is always talking about how good she is. Therefore, it was a surprise when she didn't get asked to join the older girls, but I'm guessing it has to do with the fact that they think her best chances of winning are in her own age group. Dance teams, like most teams, have a lot of politics and strategy going on behind the scenes.

However, Jess is at the studio a lot, so that's cool. I know she's Brad's girlfriend, but I just can't help the fact that my heart skips a beat every time I see her. Actually, even thinking about seeing her puts a pep in my step a little as Marc and I make our way into the studio and past the moms who are sitting in the waiting area, either talking, texting, reading, or playing games on their phones. Parents aren't really that different from us kids in some ways.

I ask Miss Julie where Jill is, and she says she is in dance room B, so we note the letters on each door as we pass A, and then step up to the door marked B.

Right before we are about to walk in, I hear music playing, so I know I need to open the door as quietly and carefully as I can. It is Lisa Loeb's "Stay," which means Jill is dancing—I have heard that song like a million times at our house now.

Marc and I quietly sneak into the room and try to make our way over to where Jess is sitting. I see there is room on one side of her, so I point to the spot and sit. Marc falls in and just stands behind me. I appreciate him not putting up a fight for the last seat, but he knows how I feel about Jess.

There's a new girl who I don't know sitting next to me, giving me the side-eyes. I guess she didn't leave that space next to Jess thinking that someone would sit there. *Oh well.*

I kind of pay attention to Jill while peeking at Jess from the corner of my eye. She looks so amazing, even if it looks like she just got done working out. That said, there is something magical about the way Jill is moving. I'm suddenly super proud of her. Everyone in this room has complete attention on Jill's every move. *Nicely done, sis.*

I don't really know all the moves, but I know one thing is certain—I couldn't do them or even anything that resembled it. No way.

As the song comes to an end, Jill stretches out and lands in the splits, which looks great and super painful at the same time, but she is all smiles. The whole room stands, and as the girl giving me the side-eyes stands, I hear a loud rip then a screech in my ear. *Uh oh*, I stepped on her dance outfit. This is not good.

Thinking quickly, I think of a rhyme and say it under my breath so nobody could possibly hear, especially with all of the clapping for Jill.

"May the clothes that are under my feet
Be repaired and wholly complete."

I don't think anybody heard that.

The girl sitting next to me fumes as she balls up the outfit and shoves it forcefully into her dance bag.

After she gets done clapping, Jess turns around and leans over to talk to the angry girl. "Darla, this is Jon, and that's Marc behind him. They are both in our class at Grinwell."

Ah, the mean girl's name is Darla.

She is apparently not interested in meeting us since she says, "Goodbye, Jess. I have to go. My dad is waiting." She turns and gives me one more look that I think could possibly be lethal then whips around and heads for the door.

Once she is gone, I turn to talk to Jess, but she is already deep in a conversation with someone else, talking about Jill. I guess that window of opportunity is shut now. I look at Marc, who just shrugs.

Jill sees us and, after saying goodbye to Miss Sally, she collects her things in her dance bag and walks over to us. "Hey, Jon, where's Mom?"

"Her and Dad were running late, so she asked me to swing by to pick you up. Ready?"

She looks down for a minute. I'm pretty sure she is a little bummed that Mom and Dad didn't get to see her rehearsal and how everyone responded. Then she quickly snaps to it with a smile and nods.

I offer a wave in Jess's direction, but she doesn't see it, so I just pretend to smooth out my hair and turn to head to the Corolla. *Smooth, Jon, real smooth.*

Marc laughs under his breath and shakes his head.

Great, he saw. I expect I'll be hearing about that later.

The Stairs

Darla

WHEN I GET OUT TO THE parking lot, I see Dad parked in his usual spot. Boy, is he a creature of habit or what? He always parks in the far corner of the lot. I guess it's smart, since I always know where to look for him.

I am so mad right now that my costume just got ripped that it's a good thing I don't have to think about where I'm going. I do my best but fail at not stomping over to the car.

Dad is already in the passenger side, clearly catching a quick nap, as I open the back door on the driver's side and throw my stuff in, probably a little too forcefully, since it causes Dad to jump, fully awake and looking at me all crazy-eyed. You know how you look when someone wakes you up unexpectantly.

As soon as he sees it's me and has a second to collect his thoughts and get his bearings, he says, "Hi, darlin', rough practice?"

I just let out a rumbling *hmph* as I get into the driver's side and slam the door.

"Darlin', you can't drive when you're mad. Tell me what happened, and let's calm you down."

That's the last thing I want to do right now. I am about halfway between white-hot anger and bursting into tears. I know I cannot avoid this, though, and I know he's right, so I say, "That *boy*!" I unintentionally pause and roll my eyes, and apparently for a little too long.

"Boy? Justin or Aiden?" he asks.

There are only two boys on our dance team, so Dad naturally jumps to the conclusion that they were involved.

"No, no, not a boy from the dance team. This was some boy who knows Jess and sat between us."

Another pause, and then Dad asks, "Did that bother you?"

I am completely over that, so I say, "Oh no, that's not it, either. When we got done watching a dance that Miss Sally wanted us to watch, we all stood up to clap for Jill, and this boy was on my dance costume, and ... and he ... he *ripped it! Hmph*!"

I have no idea why, but Dad starts laughing hysterically. He has a good old belly laugh going, enough so that he has tears in his eyes. As soon as that subsides, he says, "Is that all?"

Of course, by the time he gets to that, I'm already laughing, as well.

He's right; I was making a big deal out of it for probably no reason. At the same time, I'm pretty sure Mother isn't going to react that way when we get home. So, now my thoughts turn to what her reaction will be.

On the drive home, Dad tells me a bit about his day and some ideas he has for the farm. I don't really know what he is saying all of the time, but it's just nice to hear his voice, and he's not really looking for advice from me, just someone to talk with. He usually works things out on his own through those conversations.

It's a nice, relaxing drive, and I almost forget about my costume until we get home and I reach for my dance bag. Great, now the hard part. I'm going to have to tell Mother what happened, but I don't really want to deal with it right now. I just calmed down.

I know what she is going to say. "*You need to take better care of your things. It's not the boy's fault that you didn't have your costume tucked in your bag, now is it?*"

I decide for a different plan of action. So, as soon as I get in the door, I drop my bag and head for the stairs as quickly as possible. This is apparently too obvious, though, because I don't even reach the top stair before Mother yells up them, "Get back down here, young lady! You don't just plop your bag down and run to your room."

As soon as I force myself slowly back down the stairs, Mother knows something is up.

"What happened?"

I start to tear up a little, just because I know how disappointed she's going to be. Then I tell her that dance class went like normal with Miss Sally being as tough on us as normal. The team seems to look solid at least, from my perspective. I then get through the events after class as quickly as possible, explaining about Jill and how Miss Sally wanted us to all watch and feel the emotion of her dance. By this point, I have a tear working its way down my cheek as I tell her that my dance costume was partially in my lap and dragging on the floor a bit. And how, as I went to stand up, a boy next to me stepped on my costume, and I heard it rip.

Mother doesn't let me say anything else before she asks, "Where is it?"

I just point to my bag and put my head down for what I'm sure is coming next.

She unzips the bag, and I can't even look at her.

"Darla, it's fine. I don't see anything wrong with it at all."

I look up, completely surprised. "I heard it rip, Mother!"

"Don't be so dramatic. It's fine. Maybe it's a good lesson, though, to take better care of your things." There it is. I knew it was coming. Although, she's not wrong, so I just nod my head.

"Yes ma'am."

She seems satisfied with this response and just proceeds to make sure nothing needs to be thrown into the wash.

"You know you should tell me everything, right? It's important that you don't avoid telling me something, especially if you think I might get angry about it. If I find out after the fact, I'll be much more upset than if you just come out with it right away. Okay?"

I nod my head to show I understand and just offer up an, "I'm sorry, Mother."

She walks over and gives me a quick side hug. "I'm glad that the team is looking good. I have dinner ready in the kitchen. I'm sure you're hungry, but you can go upstairs if you want."

She's right; I am starving. So, I head in the direction of the kitchen with Mother and Dad following me.

I'm still baffled by how my costume wasn't ripped, but relieved and thankful that the whole thing was uneventful. That went differently than I thought it would for sure.

Animals and More Plants

Jon

AS SOON AS WE GET TO the car, Jill makes a move to get in the front passenger side and Marc gives a look, suggesting that I should do something about this.

I sigh. "Jill, you know the drill." Then I make a fist, stick my thumb out, and point to the back seat.

She lets out a breath of protest then switches to the back door and slumps into the back seat, defeated.

Marc gives me a look with a wave of approval then puts his hand through his hair like I just did to Jess. There it is.

I head this off by saying, "Shut up. Not a word."

He laughs then gets into the passenger seat with a huge smile on his face.

I get behind the wheel, shaking my head and smiling back. *Good one, Marc, I'll give you that.*

We drive the rest of the way home, and when we get there, we see that Mom, Dad, and Grandpa are all home now, with their cars in the drive. I pull the Corolla in, and now the driveway is officially at capacity.

Jill heads in first, probably to complain to Mom and Dad about always being the third wheel and sitting in the back seat. Marc and I make our way inside and over to the game room. It's time to get our battle on.

Just after we get the game box fired up, we hear Mom calling from the kitchen, "Boys, we picked up dinner on the way home. Come and get it!"

Marc and I get washed up then head to the kitchen for dinner and to hear about the events of the day from everyone. Marc tells everyone about Mr. Whiskers and how tore up Mr. Lemke was to see what happened to him.

"That was nice of you boys to bring Mr. Whiskers to him so he could say goodbye," Mom says.

Everyone agrees.

Grandpa gives Marc and I a quick look, and I know he is wondering what else we might have done that we left out for the benefit of everyone else at the table. I just nod in his direction and point to my eyes, and Grandpa gives a nod back. I'm sure we will talk about this after dinner.

Jill talks about how Miss Sally asked her to dance for everyone, and you could almost see the twinkle in my parents' eyes. They were beaming with pride.

"That's awesome, Jill," Dad says. "You are doing such a great job. Keep up the hard work, and see? It really does pay off."

Jill nods in approval and says, "Yes, Dad, I will. You know I will."

With that, we all clean up dinner, and then Grandpa pulls Marc and I aside and down to the basement to talk.

As soon as we get to some semblance of privacy, Grandpa says, "So, tell me everything you saw."

I described the dog, the red sports car, and the license plate to him.

Grandpa nods in approval. "That's quite the gift, Jon. That level of detail will prove to be incredibly useful." He then warns Marc, as I did, of how this needs to be kept quiet and that he should also be on alert to make sure nobody is around to see or hear one of these encounters.

Marc nods in agreement, happy to have been given a task. Then Grandpa switches back to one of the next lessons.

In our family, we have a special book that has been handed down for teaching the Bragi ways. Since I am in the Scouts, I compare it a lot to the way we earn merit badges on our way to Eagle Scout. That's a goal Marc and I are also both working on. It's a bit more than that, though, as we explore which of the powers of Bragi are within me and how prevalent they are. Lately, we have been working a lot. Grandpa reminds us that we will be covering a bunch of these in our upcoming camping trip with the Scouts.

As we look through the book, I explain to Marc about how Bragi rhymes work. The writings in the book are more of a construct for a rhyme to explore. We don't have specific sayings that we say. What we have is a general direction or something one of us has noted that we can do. Take for instance when I looked into Mr. Whisker's eyes of blue. The color of the eyes is different for each animal so, in the book, it just mentions looking into their eyes and asking for the honor of being able to see what they saw in some way. It's up to each Bragi then to take it from there.

Sometimes we find that we either don't have one of the abilities or it's also possible we aren't following the basic premise of the rhyme and just need to practice or find our own way of tapping into the power. It makes it more difficult in many ways, but it is highly personal. It's also a reason why we have to practice so much.

Speaking of practicing, Grandpa has tasked us with going through the book to determine which of the next concepts we want to test that will be much easier to attempt when we are on the camping trip surrounded by nature at Harmony Grove. There are so many interesting ones for tracking using a compass and for manipulating plants and wildlife. We make a list that is much larger than we are likely to be able to pull off in one trip, but it's better to have too many than not enough. We also don't really know how much free time we will end up having.

Marc and I are also keenly aware of which merit badges we are going to attempt to make progress on with this trip. You see, we only have about a year and a half left to get Eagle Scout, which means we have a tight schedule to stay on, and camping trips are an integral part of getting the badges we need. Needless to say, this Scout outing is important in many different ways. We cannot wait to go! It will surely be the highlight of our summer.

Wrestling

Darla

DINNER WAS SIMPLE, but I was famished, so it was perfect. Mother made a big pot of fettuccine alfredo, and all of us had a couple of platefuls. There's something about twirling those long strands of pasta and sucking it up that is so satisfying. Don't get me wrong, it tastes good, too. But, for me, half the fun of it is how you eat it.

As soon as we were full beyond comfort, a conversation started up. You see we don't talk much while eating. We also don't drink much. We wait until we have finished.

As we sat there, reflecting on the day's events, I remembered that Jess had been talking about cheer again, so I thought I would bring that up. I told Mother and Dad how Jess was going on and on about how she would help me learn the cheers in advance so that, when I tryout, I'll have everything down perfectly.

Mother says, "Isn't that nice of her? I think it would be so great for you to jump right in and get involved at your new school."

I agree, but cheer isn't exactly what I have in mind.

I pause for a minute, not sure if I want to bring it up, but I figure I might as well.

"Mother, I'm not really interested in cheer. I think I want to try something new."

She looks surprised as she says, "I see. What did you have in mind, if not cheer?"

"Well, Grinwell has a lot more options than Blue Hill, and I want to do something different."

She can tell I'm avoiding answering, so she raises her voice. "What would you like to try then, Darla? Just come out with it already."

I build up my courage then blurt out, "Wrestling!"

My mother gasps and shakes her head. "I don't know, Darla. That's not very ladylike. And, do they even have a wrestling team for girls?"

"Mother, it's a whole new world now. You know girls are allowed to wrestle boys, and I think, with the training I've had, I might be really good at it."

I can tell she's poised for battle on this issue as she pauses before delivering what I am sure is about to be a zillion reasons why this is a bad idea, when Dad surprisingly clears his throat and says, "Darlin', I think that is a fine idea. I'm sure the jiu-jitsu training you've had will come in handy in wrestling. Those boys better watch out!"

My mother gives Dad "the look." Without a doubt, they are going to have a discussion about this later.

When we lived in West Des Moines, Dad was super busy with work, but the one thing we did together was jiu-jitsu classes at the local Gracie academy. Both of us were super excited when we made it to blue belt. That doesn't sound like much, but it takes a long time to advance belts in jiu-jitsu.

While wrestling is different in lots of ways, it's like jiu-jitsu from a mental strategy perspective. You have to be highly aware of your position at all times. One of our favorite sayings was "position before submission." That just means it's important to make sure you are where you need to be before you attempt to submit your opponent. In wrestling terms, it would be similar, but instead of submitting your opponent, you are looking to pin them. In addition, the flexibility that I have worked on for years in dance is a huge advantage, as well, because uncomfortable positions are something I'm used to at this point.

I remember one of the classes, back in West Des Moines, some of the boys wouldn't roll with me. My instructor saw what was happening and had an impromptu tournament where each of us were paired up.

We all rolled, and I ended up making it to the finals at the end of the day. I got beaten by a brown belt, but I made it through all the rest of the class to get there. After that, no one ever hesitated to roll with me again.

I'm sure wrestling will be a bit like that. Sometimes you just have to suck it up and prove yourself. However, I am willing to bet that, once they see what I can do, they will accept me just like the jiu-jitsu guys did. In the end, we all want to win, and working with the best is the only way to become the best.

With Dad's support, the issue is dropped ... at least for now.

After dinner, Dad and I clean up since Mother did the cooking. That's the rule in our house—whoever cooks doesn't have to do the dishes. I load the dishwasher after Dad rinses the dishes off.

When we are done, he turns to me and says, "Don't worry about wrestling, darlin'. I'll talk to your mom. If it matters to you, you should go for it."

I can't resist giving Dad a hug and saying, "Thank you."

I know he doesn't like to contradict Mother, yet he was smart enough to jump in before Mother laid down her decision, so he wasn't technically contradicting her; he just beat her to the punch. That left it on her to "hold the line."

They have an agreement to support each other, at least in front of me. Of course, I'm fully aware of that. That was big, though, and I appreciate it. I owe him yet another one.

We run through the rest of the chores, taking out the garbage from each room, emptying waste baskets. We then quickly mop up the kitchen, dust, and sweep the hardwood floors. All of us do the work, and we do it every night. Every. Single. Night. It seems completely unnecessary, but I do have to admit it is really nice to have a super clean home every day. Nothing is out of place in our house, at least not for long. We stay on top of it, and it's not a bother; it's just one of those things we do.

After we finish up for the night, it's time to get cleaned up and head to bed. This has been quite an exhausting day, and we have to get up early to start work on the farm. All of us have tasks, and I am no exception. So, I enjoy a quick, warm shower then crawl under the covers to drift off into a nice, deep sleep.

Police Scanner

Jon

THE NEXT DAY, I WOKE up without suffering through the usual nightmare, which was a relief. That was one of the best sleeps I've had in days.

Marc slept over again, because we're up curating a list of Bragi abilities we want to test. We always have discussions over what will be more interesting to know versus what will be more useful. Marc is usually more into the bigger things, like manipulating elements—ie. the water at the lake. I'm more interested in practical things, like determining whether a wild berry is poisonous or not. There are other ways to find some of these things out, but it's still a useful talent to have, especially given that we're going camping several times as we work toward Eagle Scout. The more self-sufficient we can become, and the more we know about nature, the better, from my perspective.

We finally come up with a list and present it to Grandpa, who reads through it, stroking his beard and mostly nodding with a couple of head shakes for no. The list then gets trimmed down, with most of the ones Marc wanted eliminated, and then Grandpa says he will start working on a plan to get everything done while we're at Harmony Grove.

In addition to deciding on my Bragi list of activities, we also have to decide what Boy Scout badge we want to work toward for this camping trip. For now, we have narrowed it down to cooking, camping, or hiking badge. We may work on requirements for more than one badge; it just depends on what the other guys are doing and which leader is running each of those at our camp. There are thirteen merit badges needed for Eagle Scouts and, as of right now, we need to try to knock down about one per month, if possible. We have to be careful to not overextend, though, wanting to leave time for Bragi training with Grandpa. This is going to be a challenge to do, but thankfully, Grandpa is able to go along. Usually, Dad goes, but since Grandpa is here, Dad is sitting this one out. I'll miss him, and I know he'll miss going, but it sure is a great excuse for us to experiment with my abilities and try to level those up. For Dad and Mom, they think it's also a great opportunity for Grandpa to get to know me better, although Grandpa knows me better than they realize.

Next up for Marc and I is some side work that we have lined up to pay for gas for the Corolla and for the next releases of our favorite video games. This year, we decided to put our lawn mowers to use for a neighborhood mowing business. Most of the jobs are pretty small and only take thirty minutes to an hour to complete.

The first job today is our next-door neighbors', the Wellington twins. They are about seventy-five years young, as they constantly remind us, and they are quite the pair. Both retired schoolteachers from Grinwell Elementary School, they still believe in firm discipline, which apparently extends to their yard workers. Every time we mow their yard, one of them will complain about something we do. Usually, it's a few lines we make that are not perfectly straight that need to be corrected. Of course, every time that happens, they don't talk to us; they call one of our mothers. They usually start with mine, mainly because she's significantly easier to reach than Marc's mother. Many times, before we get to the next house, this has run full circle, and Mom is sending us back to the Wellingtons to "finish the job right."

Once we finish with the Wellingtons *again*, we head over to the church to do that yard. The church is our main job actually, since it will take three to four hours to finish by the time we get done mowing, trimming, and edging. It's a good thing it's the last job of the day, since we are usually drenched in sweat and ready to call it a day after that one.

We ride our mowers back to our houses, which takes quite a while in and of itself. It used to be fun, but now that I can drive, it's significantly less fun. However, we have to get the mowers and equipment back home somehow, and without a truck, we have no other options. We certainly are not going to be able to use the Corolla to get the equipment from job to job. Hmm ... Maybe I can somehow get a trailer that the Corolla can pull. Nah. This is just fine. It's not like Grinwell is huge. Plus, this way, Marc gets to ride his own mower, as well.

Marc and I are the same age, but he doesn't have a car yet. Frankly, he hasn't really shown any interest in even getting his driver's license. He figures he doesn't need to bother if he doesn't have a car and I can take him basically wherever we need to go. What's the point?

I get it. Sort of. Personally, I couldn't wait to get my license. Whether I was driving a family car or my own was totally irrelevant to me. To me, a driver's license symbolizes something more significant, a certain level of independence that nothing else can quite match.

After we get back and get cleaned up a little, we decide to put some of that gas money to good use and jump in the Corolla. In the late afternoon, or early evening, we like to go for a drive and listen to the police scanner. The idea is to see if anything comes up where we might be able to help. But, since the incident with the Lockes, nothing at all has happened. It's usually just people needing help with something or another at their house, and the local police being sent out to assist.

After listening in for about an hour, our attention turns to the appetite we built up.

"Why don't you use your Bragi powers to get us some burgers or something like that?" Marc says in all seriousness.

"You know that's against the rules and is no way worth the risk. Let's just head to the bowling alley and meet up with whoever is there."

So, that's what we do, and to no surprise, we see lots of cars that we recognize. I wonder if Jess is here. A quick glance around, and I see Brad is, so I assume Jess is, too. Where one goes, so does the other.

Oh well, time to fill up on burgers, fries, and their signature item—a thick, creamy strawberry shake.

Bowling

Darla

I WOKE UP TO THE FAMILIAR sound of a rooster crowing and stretch my arms as I realize it is already time to get up. For some reason, it doesn't seem like it should be morning already, but there is no time like now to start the day.

I jump into my work clothes so I can help Dad out then head downstairs to join my parents.

As I start down the stairs, I can smell a fresh pot of coffee brewing and the familiar scent of bacon and eggs wafting up the stairs and filling my lungs. My stomach gives a few short rumbles of approval. I can already taste the bacon as my mouth starts to water. Yep, this is the absolute best way to start the day! I also know where these eggs came from, because I am about to go out to collect more. Breakfast first, work second.

As I reach the kitchen, I see Mother and Dad already at the table, eating breakfast. Dad is reading the paper while the local news is blasting from the TV.

I grab a plate from the cupboard, dish up some breakfast, and then take my usual seat on the side of the table that faces a great view of the sunrise.

As soon as I am seated, Dad says, "Morning, darlin'."

I reply with a warm, "Morning," back.

Dad continues, "As soon as you're done collecting the eggs, I need you to meet me over by the barn so we can do some work on the fence line today. One of the cows must have broken through. Thankfully, none of them are missing so we don't have to hunt them down today."

Our farm is basically Old MacDonald's farm. We have chickens, cows, pigs, horses, dogs, and, of course, we grow hay for our feed, corn, and soybeans. This keeps us quite busy. We just got done detasseling the corn fields a week and a half ago. We got as many Blue Hill kids as we could to come out and help. Surprisingly, we made quick work of the fields. That is such a sweaty job, and it is so tedious that you dream of pulling tassels in your sleep every night for a week. You might even wake up with your hands in the air, pulling away.

After we clean up breakfast, I tend to the chickens. We only have about thirty in our coop and about fifteen nesting boxes to check but, for some reason, they all like to use the same nesting box, so it doesn't take long to collect the eggs. Then I check their food and water and clean the pen before taking the eggs to Mother then heading back out to meet Dad at the fence.

He greets me with, "Okay, darlin', I want to try to make sure we get everything all patched up before you head out next week."

Oh yeah, our trip is next week.

My heart skips a beat. I am really looking forward to this trip. It's going to be so different and a great chance for Jenny, Sam, Taylor, and I to have some fun. It's our big outing for the summer. Yeah, I have Nationals for dance, but this is our *big* outing as a group. No doubt this will be how we answer the inevitable first day of school question of "What did you do this summer?" Teachers always like to ask us that on the first day. It will especially be true this year with the schools consolidating. The teachers won't know us, and I'm sure they will try to "help" us all integrate and get acquainted. The last we heard, none of the teachers from Blue Hill were offered positions at Grinwell for the fall. Such a shame.

After working the fields and having a great lunchbreak at noon with my dad, I was ready to spend some time with my friends. While we were still working, I asked Dad if I could borrow the car to take Jenny with me to Grinwell to meet up with Jess. Jess had texted, wanting to introduce us to some of her friends and, apparently, this is the night "everyone who is anyone" is going to be at the bowling alley. I'm not that worried about it, but I'm sure Jenny would appreciate getting to meet some of our new classmates.

When we get back to the house Dad runs it by Mother, and we get the official approval, because Mother really, *really* likes Jess and her family. So, I get cleaned up since, well, it's rough to get people to talk to you when you smell a bit like a farm animal, and that's putting it politely.

I change into casual clothes that I know will pass the mother test—a bright yellow shirt with perfectly white capris, a fine summer outfit. Then I say goodbye to Dad and Mother with a nod of approval from her as I grab the car keys and head out the door to make my way over to pick up Jenny.

Jenny practically comes running out of her house she's so excited to be going to meet Jess. I have talked about Jess quite a bit since we are doing so much together with dance, especially with working on our duet. We have gotten really close, and Jenny knows that and isn't jealous at all. She just wants to join in on the fun and is anxious to get to know Jess, too.

Jenny is a beautiful person but has always had some weight issues that she has struggled with and sometimes is a bit self-conscious about it.

When she gets to the car, she asks, "Well, how do I look?" She does a model-like turn then opens the car door and climbs inside.

I reply the only way one possibly can to an entrance like that, "You look fab-u-lous!"

We turn on our favorite, and the only, country music station in our area as we make our way to Grinwell to pick up Jess.

When we get to her house, she is much more reserved when she makes her way to the car.

Jenny and I get out to meet her before she reaches the car, and I make the official introductions. "Jenny, this is Jess. Jess, this is my best friend, Jenny." I can see a little smile from Jenny. She knows she's my best friend, but it's always great to hear it.

Jess and Jenny give each other a quick hug, and then Jess says, "It's so great to meet you! Darla has told me so much about you."

"And she has told me a bunch about you, as well," Jenny responds. "I feel like we are already great friends!"

Jess smiles. "Let's head over to the bowling alley. Brad is already there and says that tons of our friends are there already."

We all pile back into the car, with Jess taking the passenger seat and Jenny jumping into the back. She pokes her head through the middle of the front seat to see everything and be a part of the action.

We pull up to the bowling alley, and Jess's eyes light up, excited enough for all three of us.

When we head inside, everyone seems to know Jess, and we get introduced to so many people that my head is spinning. I am positive I will not remember any of their names.

Jess then makes her way to Brad, who is bowling with some large boys who, no doubt, are part of the football team.

When we get up to them, Jess says, "Darla, Jenny, this is Brad and his posse. Guys, this is Darla and Jenny." We all exchange greetings.

"Do you girls bowl or do you want to watch us?" Brad asks.

I jumped straight in and say, "Sure, we do, and I bet we can beat you guys. What do you say boys versus girls. Loser buys dinner?"

Jess and Jenny look at me as Brad says, "You're on!"

He picks two of his friends, and then we start the hunt for bowling shoes, balls, and take our places around the scoring table. I'm pretty sure Jess and Jenny think I'm crazy, but I'm actually really good at bowling, as they all quickly find out.

We struggle a bit. Jess and Jenny are not as good as I would have expected. I probably should have asked them before dragging them into this, but it's all good fun, anyway. Surprisingly, Brad's friends aren't that great, either. They show their frustration with the "stupid pins, balls, etc."

We get through nine frames, and the score is close. It's down to Brad and me to determine the winner.

Brad gets a spare and picks up nine pins on his third ball, which means I have to make a turkey to win. I roll the first strike, and the buzz starts. Then I throw the second strike, and all eyes in the bowling alley are on me. I finish off my task when the last ball hooks right but somehow manages to knock down all the pins. I'm stunned that worked but cover it up by quickly declaring, "Losers buy dinner!"

Brad simply shrugs and extends his hand in the direction of the food counter as the girls, and I celebrate by teasing Brad and his friends on the way over to collect our burgers and fries.

The Shake

Jon

AS THE ELECTRONIC FRONT door slides open with a screech, the aroma of the bowling alley hits us. It's a unique smell that I believe anyone could pick out if they have ever been here. You could blindfold them, and then walk them inside, and they would know immediately they were in the bowling alley. It doesn't smell bad, but it also doesn't smell good. It just ... smells.

We say hello to the crowd at the front that are playing shuffleboard and pool but mostly just chatting with each other, trying to look cool. Then, as we reach the bowling lanes, my attention is completely captured by Jess. She is oddly bowling with a couple of other girls, one of them being the mean girl from dance the other day whose name I have forgotten, and someone I have never seen. This only surprises me because Jess *never* bowls. Tonight, though the girls are apparently bowling against Brad and a couple of his football buddies. Now that is *not* surprising—those guys seem to do everything together.

We stand and watch for a few frames. The mean girl is decent, but the other two are struggling to say the least. Poor Jess. I can't bear to watch any more of this, so I motion to Marc and ask, "Are you ready to order our food?"

He nods in complete agreement. "I was ready when we walked in the door."

Marc and I are hungrier than normal, so we order two double cheeseburgers, fries, and shakes. I ordered a strawberry shake, and Marc ordered chocolate, which has been his favorite since forever. Then we grab a seat and continue watching the girls versus boys showdown while we wait for our food.

Despite a few gutter balls on each side, this is turning out to be a close game. In fact, everyone is starting to gather around them as it goes into the nineth frame. Having a large crowd watching doesn't seem to shake either team. I guess they all are used to the attention, whether it's football or dance. They are all prepared to be the center of attention.

We all watch until it gets to down to Brad and the mean girl. Brad adds some pressure by picking up a spare in the tenth frame and almost gets a strike with his third ball. The mean girl will have to get a strike with each of her last three balls to win.

She gets one strike, and a buzz goes through the whole place as people cheer for one side or the other. The crowd seems pretty evenly split.

The mean girl gets a second strike, and now I feel like I have a vested interest in helping this end with a win for Jess. As mean girl winds up to deliver her final ball, I let out a rhyme with my head down and under my breath.

"Let this bowling ball strike all the pins,
No matter how it is thrown,
Make sure that this girl wins."

Marc raises a brow, surprised that I decided to risk a rhyme with so many people watching. At the same time, he is now also keenly interested in the outcome of this game.

The mean girl sets, takes a few steps forward, lowers the ball, and slips on the floor a bit as she releases it. The ball starts off heading for the gutter then the magic kicks in and it spins to significantly shift course, curving back toward the center in a way that is surely going to have people talking.

Everyone gasps then starts cheering as all the pins drop and the girls win. The place erupts in cheers.

I look over at Marc. who is shaking his head but smiling at the same time.

"That was kind of fun," he says. "Our food is ready. If you're done taking risks, Romeo, why don't you go pick it up at the counter?"

I shrug. He's not wrong.

So, they have somehow decided to give us two trays instead of putting everything on one. I guess they just expected us to both pick up our own food. I think about waving Marc over then decide to go for the balancing act. I put a hand under each tray and pick them up slowly like a professional waiter. So far so good. This isn't too bad. I turn to move toward Marc ... and slam straight into mean girl. Of course, the tray of food goes crashing down, and the girl is now wearing my entire meal, strawberry milkshake and all.

She lets out a screech that can only be described as supersonic, followed by a notable growl combined with a grunt. What was that?

I immediately start saying, "I'm sorry, I'm sorry, I'm so sorry." By the time I get to the third one, she has already grabbed what's left of my shake and dumps it on the top of my head. Of course, everyone thinks that is hilarious and starts laughing immediately.

I mumble a quick rhyme, super low so nobody can hear.

"May the outfit that I just ruined
Become perfectly clean
After it goes through a cycle in the washing machine."

I think it's important to try to limit the damage my clumsiness can cause. I don't mind everyone laughing at me, but I really don't like putting anyone out, especially for my own bad decisions.

I try to help her up, but she swats my hand away and starts yelling at me. I don't really blame her, but man, this girl has quite the list of creative names for me between the "What is with you?" and other angry questions.

At this point, my face is completely red, and I look up at Jess, who is also obviously not happy with me but more focused on helping her friend. She grabs her hand, and all three of the girls head in the direction of the ladies' room.

Brad then says, "Smooth move, Bragg!"

Everyone laughs again, of course.

By now, Marc has made his way over and is shoving me toward the door. "Let's get out of here."

I wholeheartedly agree and can't get out of that bowling alley fast enough.

As soon as we get to the Corolla, Marc starts laughing hysterically, and I glare at him before it hits me. *Ha, that was something!*

Before I know it, we are both in the car, laughing hard as we pull out of the parking lot.

"That went from amazing, to embarrassing, and then back to amazing. Why did you help that girl out?"

I think about it for a minute then shrug. "I wanted Jess to win."

He nods. "Yeah, I figured that much out. But I was talking about the clothes. I saw you whispering something and mouth the word *outfit*."

I guess maybe I wasn't as subtle with that one as I thought.

"You saw that?"

"Yeah, but I watch for stuff like that. There's no way anyone else noticed."

Whew. I need to be more careful. That was a little sloppy.

We sit in silence for a couple of minutes, and then Marc says, "You know you owe me dinner still, right? I'm starving."

With that, we head back to my place to scrounge for food. I think I've done enough damage around town for one night.

Oh Brother

Darla

JENNY, JESS, AND I head straight to the bathroom. I feel all kinds of emotions right now. It was so great to win, and then so infuriating to get food spilled all over me.

As soon as we get inside, Jenny says, "Oh Darla, I'm so sorry."

"Why?" I ask. "You didn't spill food all over me. That spazzo did! He's the same guy that I thought ripped my costume at dance the other day!"

"Really? That's weird," Jenny says.

"Wait—what happened at dance?" Jess asks.

I explain what happened.

Jess seems a bit relieved. "Whew! I mean, I'm glad the costume is okay. That could have been really bad."

"Yeah, but what is the deal with that guy? He is a walking train wreck!"

"Oh, Jon's not a bad guy; he just has always been a bit like that," Jess says. "He's a book nerd, but a sweet guy and doesn't mean to cause trouble. It just kind of seems to follow him around."

"Sweet guy? *Hmph*!" I scoff. "Sweet like this strawberry milkshake all over me?"

Jess looks at me then at Jenny then back at me, and then we all start laughing.

When we finally regain our composure, Jess says, "I'm sorry, but that was funny. Let's get out of here and go back to my place to get you some clean clothes."

We head out and quickly move through the crowd as best we can with Jess leading the way and me in-between my girls to provide as much visual protection as possible, so everyone doesn't see the mess that I am wearing.

When we get out to the car, I grab a blanket from the trunk, not wanting to get what is on me all over my mother's seat. I'm sure she won't be happy about the blanket, but she would be way more upset if there was a mess in her car. Once that is squared away, I start up the car and head over to Jess's house.

The three of us go inside and, as soon as we do her mom says, "What do we have here? What happened to your clothes, Darla?"

After we explain, she tells Jess to grab me some sweats and a T-shirt as we head into Jess's room to hang out while her mom agrees to wash my clothes and the blanket. I sure hope this works. I would rather not have to explain this to my mother. I don't want her to have to walk me through the "taking care of my stuff" speech yet again. It's just too soon. Again, she's not wrong, but I can't handle that when it really wasn't my fault. It was all that boy!

I realize I am starting to get worked up again and just let out, "That *boy*!"

Unaware of the internal conversation I had with myself, Jess and Jenny jump a little, surprised to say the least.

"What boy? Jon?" Jess asks.

"Yes, *Jon*!"

"You know who he is, right? You know he's Jill's brother?"

"Oh brother!" I reply. "That mess of a boy is related to *Jill*?"

Jess emphatically nods. "Yep, that's Jill's brother, all right."

I am completely shocked by that. Jill is so graceful and the furthest thing from clumsy that I could imagine. I'll have to give Jill a call later, for sure.

"Wow, those two couldn't be more different. She's so graceful and put together."

Jess shrugs. "Yeah, but that's not that uncommon. Jon really is a good guy, I promise."

"Maybe so," I say, "but I don't really have any interest in running into him again. No pun intended. He has already caused me enough trouble. I sure hope your mom can get those stains out of my clothes. I don't want to have to explain any of this to my mother."

Jenny chimes in, "Yeah, her mom is super strict."

"I'm sure my mom will do the best she can," Jess says, "but it's hard to say with a bowling alley burger, fries, and milkshake."

I just roll my eyes and shake my head. *What a night!*

While we wait on the clothes, we get a tour of Jess's home. It is gorgeous! This is probably the fanciest house I have ever been inside of, with six bedrooms, five bathrooms, a game room, and a fantastic pool in the backyard that is surrounded by some impressive water features and landscaping.

"Jess, your house is amazing."

"Yeah, I'm pretty lucky," she agrees. "You can come over any time and even take a swim in the pool if you want. Really, any time."

Both Jenny and I smile. I'm pretty sure we are both thinking that a swim would be awesome right about now. It's one of those moments when you wished you had brought more with you.

Instead of swimming, we go back to Jess's room to hear more about Brad and the two other guys who we were bowling against. Jess seems to think that we made quite the impression. After all, we beat the football team, and that's certainly going to be the talk of the town. So, I guess tonight was pretty successful, other than my clothes being potentially ruined.

As I'm thinking about that, Jess's mom comes in, and I hold my breath, waiting for the results.

"Look! Literally everything came out," Jess's mom says. "I'm really surprised it was that easy! I did not expect that to come out so clean. No grease. No shake. No anything."

I am so relieved that I probably say *thank you* a million times. She just politely smiles and says, "My pleasure, sweetie."

Jess's mom is so nice. I can definitely get used to coming over here, for sure.

"I hate to be a party pooper," Jenny says, "but I have to be home in twenty minutes or my parents are surely going to ground me."

I look at my phone and cannot believe the time. "I'm sorry, Jenny. I didn't realize how late it was getting. Yeah, I need to get home, too. Thank you so much, Jess! You and your mom saved me a serious discussion tonight with my mother. You are the best!"

"No worries," Jess waves me off. "Thanks for coming to town, and thanks for beating those boys. It's going to be so much fun to tease Brad about that!"

We giggle, and then the three of us hug before Jenny and I head out the door to beat the clock back to Blue Hill before missing our curfews.

Oh Sister

Jon

AFTER MARC AND I GET done raiding the refrigerator, we head to the game room to launch an epic battle with whoever is online when we run into Jill, who doesn't look happy. Then again, that's not entirely uncommon when she sees me.

She has her arms crossed and foot tapping as we approach. Clearly, something is on her mind.

"Jon, what do you think you are doing? Are you *trying* to ruin my life, or are you just that much of a klutz?"

"Um ... I have literally no idea what you are talking about."

She shifts her weight to the other side and just nods, as if I do know what she is talking about.

After about thirty seconds, I say, "Okay, well, sis, this has been fun, but Marc and I are going to play a game."

However, Jill is not done talking. She slides over to cut off the path to the game room and says, "Oh, I don't think so, brother."

"Excuse me?"

She continues, "What you did to Darla is inexcusable! Are you trying to make me the least popular girl in the dance company? What is your problem?"

"Again, I have no idea what you're talking about. I'm not trying to do anything like that. Why do you ask?"

She seems completely offended that I don't know what she's talking about. "How can you not know? I must have seen a million posts on social media about what you did to Darla at the bowling alley."

Ah ... the light finally turns on in my head. Mean girl's name is Darla, that's right.

"Oh, Jess's friend? I didn't remember her name. I promise you, I definitely did not intend to do anything like that. It just happened. It was all a total accident. If you want, I'll be more than happy to apologize to her *again*."

Jill holds both hands up. "No, I think you've done quite enough. Why don't you just stay away from Darla?"

"Sounds like a great plan to me!" I nod. "Can Marc and I play video games now, please?"

She steps aside, and Marc and I get setup for a night of gaming.

Around ten p.m., Mom comes into the game room. "You boys need to wrap it up for the night, and Marc will have to stay at his place, because we need to leave early tomorrow for the dance competition."

"What dance competition?" I ask. "I don't normally have to go to those."

"Apparently, Jill thinks you owe her one and that you need to support their team."

I groan a little but agree. "Yeah, okay. I guess I do. I'll drive Marc home now."

We say goodbye to our buddies online then drop out of the game prematurely, which is always a travesty, but we have no choice.

As I drive Marc home, he says, "Look at the bright side, Jess will be there."

That is a really good point, and it brings an immediate smile to my face. Yeah, this is going to be just fine.

THE NEXT MORNING, EVERYONE wakes up and enjoys a light breakfast because, of course, Jill needs to eat but not eat too much. I'm not totally sure what that has to do with how much *I* eat, but I'm going to play this supporting role as well as I possibly can due to this mess-up with Mean Girl—I mean, Darla. I sure hope I don't accidentally call her Mean Girl. That would be really awkward, and I'm certain even Mom wouldn't appreciate that.

After breakfast, we all pile into the minivan and head to the convention center in Oak Falls, which is about thirty minutes from Grinwell but big enough to have a convention center for a dance competition. This isn't a major competition; it's more of a warm-up for Nationals in about a month, or something like that. I wasn't paying too much attention when Mom and Jill were talking about it.

The auditorium is like every other dance competition, in that it is dark inside and freezing cold. I'm not totally sure why it has to be so cold, but I get the darkness. After all, that is normal for any stage performance.

It's a revolving door of dances that never seems to end, and even though everything they do is actually super hard and impressive, I just cannot get into it. I like watching and supporting Jill and, of course, I like cheering on Jess, but that's only a few dances out of hundreds. Plus, it's too dark to play any games on your phone or really do much of anything without everyone knowing. So, you either doze off a little or you head out to the hallway to use your phone. In fact, I walk out there several times throughout the day, but then Mom texts me before someone from our team goes on stage. Mom is great about things like that. So much better to not have to sit through every single dance.

I bump into Jess in the hallway, and I can tell she's pretty nervous about her first dance.

"Are you going to be in there watching?" she asks.

"Of course! I wouldn't miss it." Which is absolutely the truth.

She then mentions Darla and that she knows I didn't mean to do any of those "things," which is a relief. At least someone gets me.

"Can you apologize to her for me? Because Jill has me on a tight leash."

Jess laughs at that.

I'm not entirely sure I was supposed to tell her that but, around Jess, I sometimes cannot help myself. The words just slip out. I guess I tend to say whatever comes to mind that won't make it too obvious how I really feel about her.

"Is Brad coming today?" I ask to change the subject.

Her smile slips. "I don't think so. He has a football camp, but he is going to try to make it later."

"I'm sorry to hear that." Not really.

"I mean, I totally understand. He has lots of goals, as well, and I want him to be successful, too." She smiles.

At that, Mom texts. I look down at it then tell Jess, "I better go take my seat." Oh boy, more dancing ... can't wait!

We Dance

Darla

BY THE TIME I FINALLY get home from dropping off Jenny, I am dangerously close to missing curfew, which is not something I have done yet, but Mother made it clear that I don't want to find out what will happen if I am late.

I can tell someone is up and in the living room still. I have a pretty good idea it's her. Dad is a machine and, if it's possible for him to be in bed at nine p.m. sharp, he is there, because he no doubt has a huge list of to-do items planned for the next day. He gets up at four a.m. to start his routine every day. Every. Single. Day.

I quickly double-check that everything is in order in the car then walk inside to see Mother is waiting for me.

"That was a close one, Darla."

"Yes, ma'am, I know, but I made it."

She nods. "That you did. Be sure to be up early tomorrow, as your dad has some chores for you to help with before your dance competition."

I nod in return. "Okay, Mother, sounds good."

Tomorrow is a warm-up competition for Nationals, but we are up against a rival town's company, so it's still a big deal.

As I drift off into sleep, I think about everything that happened tonight. Beating the captain of the football team felt pretty good, but only half as good as just hanging out with Jess and Jenny. Maybe this next year won't be so bad after all.

I drift off to dream of the first day of school and what it will be like. I see Jess, Brad, and his football boys, and we are all hanging out in the gym. There is a big announcement that we are all waiting to hear, and then the school alarm goes off, and it sounds eerily familiar. Wait—it can't be! *Is that my alarm clock? Did I set it wrong?*

Nope, it's time to get up, all right. I guess I feel somewhat rested. It's going to have to be enough.

We eat a quick bite of breakfast—toast with peanut butter and a glass of milk. Then we head to the fields to do our chores as quickly as possible. There's no time to waste. I need at least an hour to get cleaned up, changed, and completely prepped for dance. Miss Sally does not tolerate anything but perfection when it comes to every aspect of our hair, makeup, and attire. Everything needs to be exact and conform to company standards. I'm not too worried, though. Miss Sally doesn't have anything on my mother. She will make sure everything is as perfect as it can be before we leave the house.

As I go through the motions of my daily chores, something I could probably do in my sleep, I think about today's competition. I have done our dance routines so many times that I can do the steps in my sleep now. Each jeté, plié, and pirouette, each arabesque, brisé, relevé, and everything else that Miss Sally has taught us is streaming in my mind. Whether I am working with the chickens or walking the fence line with Dad, I see something that reminds me of what we need to do today. Pointing our toes, extending our arms, and pirouette as we let the music drive our actions. Before I know it, I am dancing through the field as if it's just a normal day in the life of a farm girl.

I catch Dad watching out of the corner of my eye, smiling and shaking his head, before I make my final jeté and nearly miss a cow patty. I can already hear him clapping and whistling like only Dad can with his infamous two fingers on the sides of his mouth salute. I politely curtsy and thank my audience before we head back to the house to get ready to go.

Mother is already shoeing me up the stairs to take a shower and get ready. My costume and everything I need for our first dance is laid out and perfectly primped.

I run around, getting ready as quickly as possible, knowing it will take Mother a while to get my hair pulled up exactly right. Miss Sally wants everything to be as consistent as possible, and that includes precisely how our hair is put up into a nice, tight bun.

I let Mother know I am ready for my dance makeover. It's not as fun as it sounds. Mother isn't delicate with her movements. It's impressive how she has found a way to make hair and makeup such an unpleasant experience, but it is exceptionally fast and efficient. Before I know it, she is done and asking me to stand up and twirl around really quickly for last looks. She then nods her approval and motions for me to follow her downstairs. No words are necessary at this point. I know the drill.

When we get in the car, I take my first glance at my cell phone and see that Jess is checking in with me. Actually, she has texted several times, including the last one in all caps. "*DARLA, R U THERE? Did you get swallowed up by a cow?*"

I shake my head. Jess is so ridiculous and always adds a farm reference when I take too long to respond.

I just quickly type back, "*No, the cows prefer perky, blonde cheerleaders. Everything is great, and I am on my way right now. See you soon!*"

This simply gets about a dozen emojis in return with several smiley faces.

I turn my attention to my parents. "Mother, do you know the order we are dancing in today?"

Mother looks up and shakes her head. "Didn't you read the email I forwarded from Miss Sally?"

I don't respond because obviously I didn't read the email.

Mother continues, "You have contemporary first, and then tap, which starts at or around noon. You won't have much time between to change, Then you have hip hop, jazz, and finally your duet with Jess. It's going to be a long day, so be ready for that, and I'm sure they're running late."

It's always a long day, so I just shrug. "I'll be ready."

As soon as we pull up to the convention center in Oak Falls, we see that we must be the last people to arrive, since there is literally no parking left. We are going to have to park in a nearby neighborhood and haul my dance gear with us as we make the long walk.

Mother and Dad could drop me off, but that's not our routine. We walk together, always. The good news is Dad takes my gear for me so all I have to do is follow and pick up the pace—Mother is the world's fastest speed walker. As soon as we get in the doors, we see the hallways are lined with girls in costumes, some stretching and others grabbing corners to work on their routines.

I say goodbye to Dad, and he gives me a quick hug, saying, "Go get 'em, darlin'!"

With an extra tight squeeze, I then go with Mother as we make our way into the changing rooms to meet up with the team.

As always when we first report, we go straight to Miss Sally to get her approval of our looks. She is busy giving Alex a hard time for her hair and makeup and pointing her in the direction of someone who can help. I feel for Alex. She lost her mom to cancer earlier this year, and I'm sure her dad is doing the best he can, but he isn't up to the standards of Miss Sally. That's just entirely uncalled for, though, to make her feel that way.

I give Alex a pat on the shoulder as we pass and head over to Miss Sally. I see the approval in her eyes before we even reach her.

"Perfect as always, Darla! Now go get stretched and ready!" No muss, no fuss.

As I join Jess, I see she is talking to Jill. I have a few words I need to say to her myself.

"So, Jill, I bumped into your brother the other day, or I should say, he bumped into me."

"I'm so sorry, Darla," Jill says. "Jess and I were just talking about my clumsy brother. He's such a goof."

I smile at her, but I also seriously mean it when I say, "Just keep him away from me, please. I cannot afford another run-in with him. Literally."

"That might be hard. He's here today, so you better be on the lookout."

I hold up my hand. "Please, he better be watching for me. I'm not messing around with that boy."

Jess thinks that's pretty funny and, for whatever reason, when she starts to laugh, we all do. I guess I'm making kind of a big deal about nothing. I mean, after all, nothing irreversible has happened, and it's not like I'm going to see him in a crowd this big. What are the odds of that?

Jess and I head over to the rest of the team and start to stretch as we prepare for the first dance. There's not much time left, so we get a move on.

We Collide

Jon

SO, MOM TEXTS ME WHEN it's time for Jill and her team to do their tap routine. That's fine. I mean, I have seen it now a hundred times. Or, at least, it seems that way. Every time looks the same to me, which I guess is a good thing.

Watching them on stage, I can't help but be insanely proud of Jill. They always feature her toward the front—a big deal. I hear her and Mom talking about it after each competition. She feels a bit bad about it and wants other girls to get a chance to be in the front, but Mom always reminds her that it isn't her decision to make, that it's all up to Miss Sally, who is only doing what she thinks is best for the team, like any other good leader. I must admit she seems to know what she's doing all right because everyone is mesmerized by Jill. Sometimes you forget there are other dancers on stage. I guess that's what happens when you have a really great dancer on the team. Then again, she's my sister. Of course, I am going to be focused on her like every other family member is focused on their dancer. That makes sense.

With that, the junior dance team is done, and we only have Jill's solo left before we can head home. I, for one, am ready to go!

Fortunately, we get to watch the senior dance teams first before Jill's solo. Normally, that wouldn't be a treat for me, but I just told Jess that I would watch, so here we go. Not surprisingly, the senior team is amazing, including Jess and her friend, the mean girl.

Like I said before, I really don't understand all the fine details of dancing, but I can tell that these girls move a lot faster and are almost entirely moving in unison. I guess there is a bigger difference between the senior and junior teams than I realized.

It's clear to me that Jess is probably the best dancer in the entire competition, which is no surprise given that it is Jess. After every dance, I make sure to cheer as loudly as I can and offer a "Way to go, Jess!"

Awkwardly, Brad ended up making it, as well, and is also cheering as aggressively. It looks like we have a cheer off going on. I say something, and then Brad attempts to top it. Brad also has his football friends with him, and I just realized that I don't have anyone with me. I really wish Marc could have come today, but he was conveniently busy with anything else he could think of to avoid coming.

For now, I decide to concede and offer a wave over to Brad and the guys as he gives a shoot and a wink over to me and mouths, "*Love you, Jon-boy.*" That never gets old. Geesh, your mom makes one comment while dropping you off at school and you are forever haunted by it.

I need a break, so I excuse myself and head to the concession area to grab a banana and a bottle of water. That's pretty much as close as they got to junk food at most dance competitions, wanting to keep things light and healthy for the dancers. Makes sense but isn't ideal for family and friends.

I take a few laps around the vendor area and look at the same dance T-shirts with no intention of buying one, but sometimes they have some interesting sayings on them. Then, as I head to a corner to cop a squat and read a book, I get grabbed from behind and lifted in the air like I'm a toddler.

Great, it's Brad and his football buddies.

"Hey, Jon-boy! Your sister is pretty good, isn't she?"

I nod and wait for whatever they plan to do next.

Surprisingly, Brad just says, "Tell her good job for me."

Nice. That was pleasant and unexpected, so I reply, "Sure thing, Brad. Thanks!"

As he walks away, he says, "Don't worry; I'll tell Jess you said she was awesome-sauce, as well, Jon-boy!"

They laugh as they head back to their seats. On the whole, that wasn't bad, and Jess was awesome, so that's fine by me.

I have been reading an English Translation of *The Poetic Edda* by Dodds. Knowing my heritage and better understanding everything surrounding it has become a bit of a passion for me. I have an insatiable appetite for it, to say the least. I am particularly intrigued by the giants and their role in Ragnarök. I am also curious as to whether or not any other lines have descendants. There must be more. I'll have to remember to ask Grandpa what he knows about that later.

Just as I am getting deep into my book, my phone buzzes. Time for Jill's solo. *Great, just great.*

I collect myself and head back to my seat just in time to hear the music start and Lisa Loeb croon "*You say, I only hear what I want to ...*" Other than the music, there is dead silence in the auditorium, all eyes on Jill.

I know I'm a guy, but there is something about that song that just digs into your brain, and you can't help but be a little enthralled by it.

Jill moves with precision and, as far as I can tell, doesn't make a single mistake. By the time the song ends, she has everyone's attention, including all the siblings that were on their iPads and phones. She gets a standing ovation, and I look over to see Mom and Dad beaming with pride. That was cool, I must admit.

As she walks off the stage, Mom and Dad pick up our things and head out into the hall so we can go find Jill.

Miss Sally is with her, giving her a big hug. Several of her friends are surrounding her, as well, all clearly excited for her.

As they leave, Jill sees us heading her way and starts to walk toward us. I can't wait and bust out in a jog to get to her first. Just as I'm about to reach her, I see someone coming out of the corner of my eye from a side corridor and then *BAM!* we collide.

It takes me a second to get my bearings, and I realize that it is—no way! It's Mean Girl *again*! She winces in pain, and I think quickly then softly whisper a health rhyme.

"May this mean girl rapidly heal
To feel as amazing as she can feel,
And may this apology seal the deal."

I immediately speak up. "I'm sorry, I'm sorry, I'm so sorry!"

Everyone is rushing over to check on us. Well, to check on her, to be honest.

Getting to her feet, she is already pointing at me. "*You!* Why is it always *you*? *Stay. Away. From. Me!*" She storms off in the opposite direction, and I feel my cheeks burning as I lower my head and try to find the nearest exit.

What is wrong with me? I keep running into that girl. I have to get out of here.

I head out to the car, even though nobody is there. At least I can be alone for a minute. I'm sure I haven't heard the last of this one. It's going to be a long drive home.

Man, I cannot wait to leave for the scouting trip and just get away from all this, with zero possibility of running into any girls. Especially *that* girl! I'm so over this situation.

Packing

Darla

JESS AND I ARE HUDDLED together, waiting for the results of the dance competition, which is always the worst part. We know we did our best, but somehow, we always seem to be surprised by one score or another. We all sit on the stage, clapping for each announcement, because that's just what we always do.

One great thing about dancers is that we at least pretend to support each other, and a majority of the time, that is completely genuine. But I am so driven to win that all I care about is our scores.

So far, we have two platinum elite scores and two platinum scores, which is great. Now we wait for the results of the duet that Jess and I performed.

Oh, here it is. They just announced the runner up for top overall duet, and it isn't us!

Before they even announce our names, Jess is already jumping on my back, and then up and down, all the way over to claim our prize. It's a ribbon, which isn't as great as a trophy or medal, but a win is a win, so I'll take it!

Our whole dance company swarms us, and I couldn't be happier. It just feels so good to win. I love it!

On the way home, Dad turns and asks if I want to stop to get ice cream to celebrate. Of course I do!

I order up a banana split because: why not? It comes out just perfect. The bananas are the perfect level of ripeness, and the ice cream is thick and creamy, exactly like it should be. This is a perfect ending to an almost perfect day. If I hadn't had a near miss with Jill's brother yet again, it would have been perfect.

That boy! There is just something so incredibly annoying about him, and not just the fact that he is the clumsiest person in the world. For some reason, I just really don't like him, and I cannot help myself. Nothing happened, though. I am totally fine, but lately, I haven't had any injuries or any problems, anyway. I just feel stronger and stronger every day, every week, and for every competition. I can really tell that all of the hours practicing dance have paid off this spring and summer.

Finishing up my banana split, Dad says, "Don't forget you need to pack tomorrow to get ready for camp."

I can barely hold my newfound excitement in as I reply, "Yes! I'm really looking forward to a few days off with Jenny!" Okay, it's official. Best. Day. Ever!

The drive home and the rest of the night fly by as I am now only thinking about getting away somewhere, anywhere really. I am exhausted, though, and I bet I'm just going to fall asleep before my head hits the ...

Before I know it, I am back at Grinwell High, and I am meeting with the principal for some reason. Apparently, there has been an accident, and one of the kids was really injured. It was during wrestling, and they are accusing me of doing something to them. What? All I did was wrestle. Then a quick flash of me putting a firm kimura on this guy and feeling pure glee about it as I hear a snap, and then the bell rings yet again. Why is the bell ringing when I was just in the principal's office? Oh yeah, of course, it's my alarm.

I reach over to shut it off. I can't shake the fact that these dreams just feel so real. That's funny, if you think about it. I'm getting in trouble at a school that I don't even go to yet, doing something that I doubt my mother is even going to let me do in the first place. Yep, that's just ridiculous. Nevertheless, it sure felt like it happened. I wonder what that boy did to deserve that? Oh well, maybe I'll dream about that another night.

The daily routine kicks in as I grab a bite, do my chores, and then head back into the house to pack. Finally, packing for my escape from this daily grind. This is going to be so much fun and so different! I have never done any sort of actual camping before, so it's going to be great to go with Jenny, Sam, and my other Blue Hill friends. It's kind of our last *hurrah* as a group, before Blue Hill High is no more and we join up with the kids at Grinwell.

I'm going to miss our little school, even if it is ancient and possibly full of asbestos. It is still *our* school.

Mother has given me the list of things to pack, and I'm sure she's going to be checking it over thoroughly, so I better not miss anything. Sleeping bag, flashlight, pillow, bug spray, and everything else on the list seems to be in order to me.

When I go downstairs, Dad gives me pointers on everything he knows about the woods, which honestly isn't even registering in my brain, but it's the thought that counts.

One last inspection of my packing from Mother, and we are making our way to the car.

As we approach our old school, I see Jenny and all my friends are already on the school bus. I sure hope Jenny saved a spot for me. I'm sure she did. Even if she didn't, everyone knows that we sit together, so this won't be a problem, I'm sure.

Mother heads over to talk to the leaders of our trip, no doubt making sure they know that I need to be careful. I have dance Nationals coming up and/or telling them that they should call her if there are any problems, as if they didn't already know that.

As soon as that is all over, Mother and Dad come over to me. Dad gives me a hug and says, "Darlin', just remember you are a Towns, and we love you no matter what. That said, make good decisions."

I grin and shake my head as I say, "I know, Dad. I will. Don't worry!"

I then say goodbye to Mother, who gives me the once-over, as if there is something wrong with my attire or something.

"What? What's wrong?" I ask.

She shrugs. "It's nothing, Darla. We'll talk about it when you get home. Have a pleasant week."

I just nod then head onto the bus. Parents, so dramatic. I'll be fine. What's the worst that could happen? A few mosquito bites? Bring it on!

Just The Boys

Jon

"RISE AND SHINE, SUNSHINE!" comes from Grandpa as I slowly wake up. It takes me a good minute or so before I spring into action as I remember today is the day we head off on our scouting trip! It really couldn't come at a better time. I'm so ready to get away for a week and to just relax and spend time with Marc and my friends.

Most of the guys in our troop are pretty similar to us. We spend a lot of time playing video games together online. It's part of why we all get along so well, I think—we get each other, and we like a lot of the same things.

I look up at Grandpa and I instantly realize that he's already fully packed and ready to go. I have some catching up to do. But, since I am a good scout, I'm always prepared for a camping trip. I have my camping locker ready to go at all times and just have to throw the essentials in this morning. Then I'll be all set.

"I have a full week of Bragi training planned, as well, for us, so we will want to get settled as quickly as possible this morning when we get to Harmony Grove. If we are lucky, we can get some rhymes in before the week officially kicks off. No time to waste!"

I nod. "Yes, sir. Marc and I won't take long to set up. We have done this a million times, so we should have plenty of time to check out the woods before the opening ceremony."

Grandpa nods with approval. "That's great, Jon. This is going to be a fun week. I'm so glad I get to do this with you. I know your dad usually goes, but this means a lot to me."

I give Grandpa a hug and tell him, "It means a lot to me, too, Grandpa. Thank *you* for coming!"

He relents and says, "You're welcome, Jon. Wouldn't miss it for the world. Now let's get down to breakfast so we can hit the road!"

Before I even hit the top of the stairs, I can tell that not only did Grandpa beat me awake this morning, but he has made his famous waffles and chicken, which means this day just couldn't get any better. When I reach the kitchen, I see that everyone is up to see us off, even Jill. That surprises me since she normally sleeps in for a long time after a dance competition.

"Good morning, boys," Mom says. "Grab a chair, and I'll fix you a plate."

Grandpa sits next to Jill, and I sit across from him, next to Dad.

Dad looks up from reading the "news" on his tablet—really, he's scrolling through social media and laughing at the latest viral videos. "Jon, we need to talk about last night. We know you just wanted to congratulate Jill and accidents happen, but you can't just run off like that. We aren't upset that you bumped into that girl, just disappointed that you ran off without making sure she was okay."

I lower my head immediately, knowing he's right. I let out a humble, "I'm sorry, Dad. I'll handle it better next time."

To which Jill says, "There better not *be* a next time, Jon."

Mom and Dad move to settle her down as I shake my head in agreement and reply, "No, you're right, Jill. I should have said that I'll make sure it doesn't happen again. I'm sorry. Is she okay?"

"Yes," Mom answers. "Her and Jess even won the top overall duet after that, so she was more than fine."

"Well, that's great!"

Jill just mumbles, "No thanks to you."

I guess I had that coming. Man, I can't wait to leave this behind me, so I eat as fast as I can and notice Grandpa is doing the same.

Mom, Dad, and Jill all stand outside and wave as Grandpa and I head off in the Corolla to pick up Marc then head to Grinwell High to catch the bus with the rest of our troop.

We don't even have to wait for Marc; he is already outside of his house and copping a squat on his scout locker, which, let's face it, is the best use of those by far.

Marc knows better than to do our normal greeting with Grandpa in the car, so he just says, "Good morning, Grandpa, Jon." Grandpa has pretty much adopted Marc as a grandson, so this is completely normal for all of us.

"Good morning, son. Let's get your gear loaded. We're running behind already."

We quickly snatch up his gear and jam it into the back seat since the trunk is totally full with what Grandpa and I brought. Then Marc squeezes into the back seat and acknowledges, "I'm in. Let's go!"

With that, we are off to meet up with our friends and start our adventure together.

On the drive over, we finalize our plans for which badges we are going to work on, subject to what the other guys are doing, and Grandpa tells us a bit more about what his plans are for training this week. We are going to be focused on becoming one with the nature around us. It makes sense, being in the woods and all. We are also going to work on some plant and vegetation rhymes, tracking rhymes, and a few others that Grandpa is holding close to his vest. Those are a surprise, and he specifically points out that they weren't on the list we gave him. Of course, now that's the only thing that I can think about.

Nicely done, Grandpa. Now my curiosity is piqued.

When we pull up to the school, we see we aren't the last to arrive, after all. We get everything loaded up on the bus then circle up with our friends to talk about what we're all planning to do this week as we wait for the rest of the troop to arrive. It's so nice to be with these guys. I'm ready for some time with just the boys.

As soon as everyone has arrived, the leaders gather us all up into a big circle to go over the rules once again. It's really the same thing every time.

Make sure you buddy up and know that you are accountable for each other.

Whenever we go anywhere, we go in groups of two or more.

We are welcome to spend time hiking, canoeing, swimming, and whatever else we can find as long as we don't run off on our own, and as long as a leader is aware of what we are doing.

It's all pretty standard operating procedures, so most of us are completely zoned out while they recount the rules, our minds drifting off to thoughts of what we're going to do first at Harmony Grove. Apparently, we aren't fooling any of the leaders since the troop leader, Skipper, finally says, "Okay, you knuckleheads, let's get on the bus and make our way to the campsite."

We all let out a yell of approval, and then we are off to Harmony Grove *finally*!

Pitching a Tent

Darla

AFTER A FAIRLY SHORT drive, we arrive at the lake. All of us grab our bags, bumping into the bus seats as we make our way out to the campsite. There is a nice, flat spot about twenty feet from the water that is clearly where the tents are going to go. You can see a large dirt area with a stone circle outline in the middle for a campfire. It hasn't rained much this summer, so the ground is nice and dry. That is good in some ways and bad in others. Either way, we make our way over to an area that is closer to the woods and on the outer ring of the circle. I like water and all, but I would rather be a little farther away from it when I'm sleeping. I'm not sure why, but I am afraid that, somehow, in the middle of the night, the water is going to jump out of its banks and make its way to my tent to soak all our things. Yeah, that's just ridiculous. Nonetheless, I'm going to just go ahead and stay as far away from it as I can.

I look at Jenny, Sam, and Taylor and ask, "How about right here? I'd like to be a bit away from the water."

Sam smiles. "Sure, Darla, this is fine."

We drop our stuff then start getting the tents out of their carrying bags. Jenny and I lay everything out on the ground then walk around, surveying it as if the tent is suddenly going to pitch itself, which would be pretty awesome but isn't happening. I have been meaning to practice this with Dad but never got around to it.

"Have you ever done this before?" I ask Jenny.

She shakes her head. "Nope, first time."

We both glance over to where Sam and Taylor are setting up their tent up. They make it look super easy.

Let's see. They are connecting these poles together like so, and then running the poles through the canvas like this. Then, when they are done, the tent is just suddenly standing up, and they poke the stakes into the ground.

I'm not sure, but I think I missed a few steps, because Jenny and I are suddenly somehow inside a collapsed tent and listening to Sam and Taylor laugh uncontrollably outside.

"Need some help, Darla?" Sam asks.

I let out a groan of surrender. "Yes, please."

There are times for stubborn pride, and then there are times to accept help. Sometimes, you just have to give in and acknowledge that you don't know everything. It's fine. I'll get over it.

Sam, Taylor, and Jenny have grown up knowing each other in Blue Hill. I am relatively new, but you wouldn't know it. We all hit it off immediately, and it feels like I have known them my whole life. That might be why I am so willing to accept their help. That's what we do—we take care of each other. I am going to miss this gang and how close we are. Time will tell if we are able to continue being such a tight knit group next year when the schools merge. I'm willing to bet that we will, though. After all, we're all going to either be riding together or hopping on the bus, depending on whether or not any of us has a car available on any given day.

I also expect that all of us from Blue Hill will hang out at lunch and, most likely, gravitate toward each other to avoid some of the awkwardness of being the outsiders at a new school. There's no question that our school was too small to hold everyone, so we understand why we have to go to Grinwell, but it seems like an unfair advantage for them to have the comfort of their own school.

With Sam and Taylor supervising, Jenny and I finally get our tent up and, surprisingly, it seems pretty sturdy. Jenny and I thank them then head inside the tent to start setting up our sleeping bags and getting as settled as one can in such a small area.

This tent is so cute. It's like we built our own little fort for just the two of us.

Jenny takes out a radio and, after playing with the dial a bit, we pick up the only station we can get out here. It's the Grinwell oldies station, so it seems like we will be enjoying the 80s all week. It doesn't really matter too much. We just need some background noise. It doesn't matter if it's Taylor Swift or The Bangles with "Walk Like an Egyptian."

We dance a little narrowly, avoiding hitting our heads on the top of the tent as we circle inside, doing our best imitation of the music video and having more fun than we have had in what feels like ages. I just want to enjoy this moment as much as possible, hanging out with my best friend, in the middle of nowhere, with the chance of being bothered by no one, especially not our parents. This week, we will be able to do whatever we want, at least in here, our little home away from home.

Jenny and I decide to grab some snacks from our sealed-up bags. We were careful to pack food in containers that won't be possible for animals to smell. That's what we were told to do, and it makes sense. The last thing we want is some animal coming in here, especially while we are sleeping, looking for some dinner.

I'm not too worried about most animals, but I am deathly afraid of snakes. Everything about them is scary, from the way their little tongues flash in and out to the way they slither across the ground. I really hope we don't see any around the camp or even when we're hiking. I have zero interest in that. In fact, my interest is below zero. No, thank you! Hard pass!

Sam and Taylor stop by and verbally say, "Knock, knock!"

We unzip the entrance as Jenny asks, "Who's there?"

We all laugh as if that is the funniest thing we have ever heard, even though it's definitely not.

Sam has to meet up with the camp leaders, so Taylor joins our snack party, and we talk about what we plan to do first, before the camp officially starts.

Harmony Grove

Jon

I GRAB A SEAT NEXT to Marc on the bus as everyone rushes in and plops their gear next to them on the first available seat. It's interesting how there aren't any seat belts on the bus, but when we are in a car, we are required to wear them. I wonder what the thinking was there? To be honest, I think that would only make riding on a bus less comfortable, but it might stop some of the guys from running around and messing with each other.

Our bus driver is one of the scout leaders, and he seems perfectly fine with the chaos that is breaking out behind him. Marc and I, however, do our best to ignore the wet willy fest and keep our heads down. I am reading one of my favorite books, *Hatchet* by Gary Paulsen. It may not be the best thing to read before spending a week in the woods, but at least we aren't going on a plane ride, right?

Marc pulls me from the book as the pilot is having a heart attack to ask, "So, what are we going to do first?"

Typical. Marc is one of those guys who is always asking what is next. It's not that the schedule has changed. I guess it's just something to say.

I humor him by saying, "Same thing as always. We will get there and set up our tent, and then I'll head to the scout patrol meeting. We can meet up with Grandpa after that to do some training. I mean, hiking."

Marc nods. "That's right. Man, I just can't wait to get there!"

"Well, we don't have too long of a drive, and we don't have much of a choice other than to relax and enjoy it."

Marc nods in agreement and, with that, I fall back into reading my book and escaping into the world of high stakes plane piloting and landing. How wild would that be to have something like that happen to you?

Just as I am falling back into a nice reading rhythm, I hear an adult clear his throat then says, "Uh, men? Excuse me, boys. *Boys! Settle down!*"

Well, I guess *someone* isn't in the mood to deal with the energy on the bus today.

He continues, "We have an important announcement to tell you boys. We will be meeting up with another troop when we get to Harmony Grove. They are from Blue Hill. It'll be a good opportunity for you to get to meet some of them before school starts up in the fall."

Well, that did the trick. Everyone settled down really fast. You literally could hear a pin drop. As a matter of fact, as if on cue, my highlighter rolls off my book and hits the floor. Then it starts rolling toward the back of the bus before I have a chance to grab it. Yeah, I am never going to see that thing again.

After what seems like an eternity but is probably only thirty seconds, everyone starts shouting out questions, like "How many of them are there?"

The leader is quickly overwhelmed and takes a second to collect himself as he puts out both hands and makes a gesture for us to settle down again. "We will find all of that out when we get there. The important thing is that we want you to know, and we expect you to be on your best behavior. You are representing our troop and all of Grinwell, so do your best to be friendly and welcoming to the Scouts from Blue Hill, got it?"

There is a unison of groans that comes from all of us.

"What's that?" the leader asks.

We all say, "Yes, sir!"

The leader then turns around, as if he didn't just drop a boulder in the middle of a calm lake, as the ripples expand and head for the shore.

I go ahead and just put my book away. There is no chance that I'm going to get in any more good reading done after *that* announcement.

Sure enough, Marc says, "Well, that was unexpected."

I nod in agreement. "I'm sure it'll be fine. They are just Scouts, like us, so it's really not any different, just more of us for games and activities. It should be fun."

Marc thinks about it for a second. "Yeah, I guess it really doesn't change anything. If anything, it'll probably be easier for us to get away from the pack."

"I'm not worried about it at all. It's going to be fine, just fine."

Meanwhile, the rest of the bus is ready to declare war on the troop from Blue Hill. Not for any particular reason. I guess they just feel like someone has crashed our party, and they want to do something about it.

They almost immediately start talking about the various pranks they want to play on the Blue Hill troop. I don't think that's a good idea. Not at all. I'm sure that all the leaders will crack down hard and fast on any of those types of "shenanigans."

It only takes about twenty minutes to get to Harmony Grove from the school, so we are already pulling up into the camp. It's one of those old dirt roads with brown, wooden signs on posts that guide you to the campsite. It's also super bumpy because the "roads" are really just two tire marks that the bus is doing its best to follow as we all bounce around inside like balls in a pinball machine as we slam up and down repeatedly into our seats. As we get closer, we get smaller, more consistent bumps, which make it fun to talk, and there is plenty of talking going on as we round the corner and catch a glimpse of several tents already pitched.

"Great, we got here last."

Before the bus even comes to a stop, everyone has stood up and is rushing to the front of the bus to get out first and claim their spot to pitch their tent. Honestly, I'm not worried about it. There will be plenty of room for all of us, and it really doesn't matter where our tent is pitched. Thankfully, Marc feels the same way, so we just hang back while everyone else rushes out the doors and starts running to throw their lockers and tents down on what they think is the best remaining spots.

There is a little pushing and shoving, and the leaders are doing their best to keep it all under control. Marc and I just look at each other and laugh. This is quite the sight to take in and some of the best people-watching I have seen in a long time.

As soon as they all settle down, Marc and I look at each other then pick our stuff up and calmly head out to claim whatever spot is remaining. Yep, this will be just fine. No big deal. In fact, we have a spot on the edge closest to the woods, which is literally perfect. We will be able to sneak out to the woods for Bragi training easily.

The Clipboard

Darla

AFTER GETTING OUR FILL of the mostly healthy super food snacks that my mother sent for me to eat, because "I have to watch my weight for dance," Jenny, Taylor, and I talk about what happens next at these camps. Taylor has been to several, and we haven't.

"Sam and the other leaders will meet and go over the plans for the week," Taylor says. "Together, they will decide the opening ceremony and all the activities we are going to do."

That gets my attention. "You mean, the trainings?"

Taylor nods. "Yes, but we also play different games for various prizes and whatnot."

"Now we're talking!" I exclaim. "What kind of games? Like sports?"

"Nah," Taylor says. "Things like a hiking challenge or passing a grapefruit without using your hands down a long line of people and back."

Jenny and I look at each other then break out in laughter.

"That sounds pretty dumb," Jenny says. "We used to do those types of things when we were in grade school."

Taylor shrugs. "Hey, you asked." With that, Taylor heads toward the zipper door as if we're being offensive. "Sam will let us know the plan when they are done."

We wave, and then it's back to only Jenny and me.

It takes all of about five minutes of staring at the tent ceiling before Jenny and I are bored to tears.

I turn to her. "Camping is dull. What should we do now?"

Jenny nods, and then we both drop our heads, deep in thought.

"We could go for a hike in the woods?" Jenny offers.

"Sure. Why not?"

We open the tent then zip it shut behind us, as if that's going to deter anyone from going in there if they want to. Then we spin around to take a look in all directions. That's when we notice there are lots and lots of tents already set up. We hear all kinds of hushed sounds coming from all of them and figure that everyone is getting settled.

We make for the densest section of trees to begin our hike. There is a wide, well-marked path in that direction and, while we feel adventurous, we know that we need to stay on the trails.

I turn to Jenny. "Okay, if we come to a fork in the trail, we are always going to take a right on the way there, and then a left on the way back, got it?"

She nods.

As we walk along the trail, we point out different trees, flowers, and lots and lots of big spider webs. Thankfully, we don't see any spiders but, deep down, I also know those webs didn't create themselves. We come across a squirrel in the middle of the trail that doesn't seem interested in moving. I expect it to make a run for it as we get closer and closer, but this little guy isn't going anywhere.

As soon as we get to it, we crouch down, and Jenny says, "Well, isn't he the cutest little guy?" She reaches out and actually pets the squirrel.

"*Jenny!*" I shout.

This startles the squirrel, who heads off the trail and up the nearest tree.

I continue, "You don't know where that thing has been. We can look, but we probably shouldn't touch."

She holds up her hand, shooing that notion away. "You worry too much. It's just a squirrel, and we know he's been right here, in these woods."

To which, I reply, "Exactly!"

By the time I say this, Jenny is already a few steps down the trail and doesn't even bother looking back. Huh, she's kind of fearless. That's unexpected.

After we get a ways into the woods, I look over and see something laying on the ground. I can't quite make it out. It's off the path and the grass is thick. I yell to Jenny, "Hold up for a minute. I think I see something." I carefully step off the trail, doing my best "tiptoe through the tulips," to avoid the weeds. Then I bend down to pick it up with two fingers, barely touching it, like you would a dead animal. "Look at *this*!"

It's a clipboard that has "*Grinwell High School*" on it.

"Boy, those Grinwell kids have already managed to one, lose stuff, and two, litter in the woods." I drop it then brush the dirt off my hands. "I guess I'll just leave that where I found it. Maybe it's part of a game or something. Who knows?"

We look up and down the trail, and I start to get a bit of a mini panic attack. I can see it in Jenny's eyes, as well.

I say it first. "Want to head back?"

She doesn't even wait. She turns around and starts running. "Last one there is a rotten egg!" With that, the race is on.

After about twenty steps, I already pass Jenny. I decide to not go too fast, though, because I would rather we stick together.

As soon as we reach the clearing, we see activity at the camp. Lots of people are out and about, and it looks like they are getting ready to go somewhere.

Jenny and I head for our tent, which basically looks like every other tent. As soon as we get there, we see that Sam and Taylor are standing outside their tent, and it looks like Sam is giving Taylor an update.

When we walk up to them, Sam says, "There you are. Where did you two go?"

"For a hike," we say, as if that is something we do all the time.

Sam and Taylor look at each other, smiling, and then Sam says, "Nice! Let me fill you in on what's going to happen next, okay?"

"Spill it!" I order. "I want to know all the details, especially about any of the games. I need to get ready to pile up some wins!"

Senior Patrol Leader

Jon

AT THIS POINT, MARC and I have put up this tent what seems like a million times. It's one of those things where we each already knows our job and don't have to say anything to each other; we just work in unison and get the tent set up in no time.

Once we have our stuff spread out inside the tent, I start to prepare for what's coming next.

The guys in the troop conspired to elect me as Senior Patrol Leader. Of course I gladly accepted that honor, even though I may not seem like the most likely candidate to plan fun activities, but I think everyone knows that I will definitely be well-prepared. I have read about my responsibilities over and over and have this down, even if it's my first real opportunity to put that knowledge into action. I cannot wait for the leaders to let us know they are ready to talk.

As if on cue, Grandpa comes over and says "We need you over in the leaders' area."

Excellent. Let's do this!

When I get over there, I see something that I was not expecting. The leaders from both the Grinwell and Blue Hill troops are sitting together around a couple of old, wood picnic tables that have been pushed together. I guess I shouldn't be surprised after the announcement on the bus but, for a minute, I'm a little disappointed, because, no doubt, some of my ideas are not going to be accepted now that we *all* have to agree on them.

I put myself in check and plant a smile on my face. Compromise. It's all about the art of compromise. I can do this. There really isn't anything that they can say or do that is going to take the fun out of this week. We are at Harmony Grove, the sun is out, the water is cool, and we are all going to have a great time.

I hear a group of birds chirping like they agree with my attitude, and then I grab a seat next to one of the Blue Hill leaders.

Our troop leader is Robert Jackson, but we all call him Skipper. He's a bit portly, so his scout leader uniform looks a bit funny, but it just makes me like him even more. He has a graying goatee and some round, wire-rimmed glasses that slide to the tip of his nose when he gets excited or nervous. I guess he must be one or the other right now since they're about to fall off his face and hit the ground at any second.

"Boys," he addresses us, "as you know, we are combining troops for this camp outing to give the Grinwell and Blue Hill scouts a good chance to get to know each other. I know this may not be what you expected, but we ask that, as leaders, you set a good example by working together all week. Sound good?"

We all say, "Yes, sir!" It seems like we have already made up our minds to make the best of this situation. In fact, this works out great for me. I will have a few less responsibilities, and that will give me more time for all things Bragi.

We go around the table, everyone introducing themselves. The patrol leader for Blue Hill is named Sam, who is a sight to behold, if I'm honest. A solid six-foot-four and must weigh over two hundred pounds, of which I think a high percentage is muscle. This guy looks like he ate a couple of our football players and has super curly, hair and a tan that clearly comes from being in the fields most of the summer. Yep, he's a big old farm boy, that's for sure. And he is certainly prepared, as he has a notebook full of things written down that closely matches my own.

As he reaches over the table to shake my hand, his hand totally swallows mine as I suddenly feel about four times smaller than when I walked over here.

"Good to meet you Jon." He has a warm smile that is welcoming.

I return his smile. "Likewise."

We plan out the opening assembly and which troop will be responsible for each part. This is a mundane task, but to us scouts, it's important since it kicks off the week. Then we talk about the various activities we all plan to do. This is where we start having to compromise. Both Sam and I have fully planned out our own events, so we end up taking turns picking the activities; one game for Grinwell, one for Blue Hill until we have everything planned out. It's a good thing that most of the activities we both planned will not be impacted by the larger number of participants.

After we have agreed on the schedule, Mr. Jackson drops this bomb. "We will be splitting the troops up into teams with some members from Blue Hill and some from Grinwell on each team. From there, you will all partner up for the various activities or complete them as a team, whatever is appropriate."

Sam and I just look at each other and offer a careless shrug in unison. It's fine.

Skipper then hands each of us a list and asks, "Do you have any other questions, boys?"

Both Sam and I intently scan the list. Of course, I'm looking for Marc's name, scanning the list using my finger.

Wait. What is this?

I slide my finger back up the list and say, "Skipper, I think there is something wrong with my list. There's a girl's name on it. Right here." I point it out to him.

Skipper sits down and looks up at me. "No, Jon, the list is correct."

Sam then says, "When Scouts BSA made the announcement that girls could join, we had a couple sign up in Blue Hill. It took a minute to get used to, but you'll really like Darla and Jenny. They are good scouts and good people. I'd vouch for them any day."

Okay, well, that's good enough for me, I guess. Wait until I tell the rest of the guys about this. The only thing I'm bummed about is Marc isn't on my list, but I'm sure he'll do fine with the Blue Hill Scouts.

Wait ...

Darla Towns? No way. It can't be!

Teams

Darla

SAM STARES AT ME, AND I can already see that he doesn't want to tell me something.

"What? How bad can it be?"

"It's not bad ... necessarily. I'm just not sure how you're going to take the news that the troops are splitting into two teams with some from Blue Hill and some from Grinwell."

Well, that's not what I had in mind at all. I really wanted to spend time with everyone from Blue Hill one last time. Then again, it's not like this is Sam's fault.

"Okay, well, at least tell me that you, Taylor, Jenny, and I are all together, right?"

He immediately looks at the ground as he says, "Well, that's mostly right. Taylor, Jenny, and I are on the same team."

I immediately react with, "What? No! I'm the only one going over to their side? Give me that list." I snatch it from him then scan down the list. I see several names that I'm familiar with, and then a bunch that I'm not who are with Sam, Taylor, and Jenny. Then I flip it over and see that the Senior Patrol Leader for Grinwell is ...

Jon Bragg?

No way! Of course it's Jill's brother. Great, just great! This is going to be awful. I wonder if it's too late to call my parents and get out of here.

I throw the paper on the ground, turn around, and head back to the tent. I don't even want to hear the rest. It's bad enough that I'm not with our group, but then to make it worse, my team is being led by that clumsy, bumbling idiot.

In the distance, I hear Jenny ask, "Is there any way we can talk to them and get Darla on our team?" I don't hear a response, but I do hear Jenny hot on my heels, so I'm guessing that the answer was negative.

In the tent, I hop into my sleeping bag and zip it all the way up as I sink down into it. I'm not much for crying, but this is about as close as I have been in a long time. I'm not sad. I'm not homesick. I am furious and about as irritated as a person can be.

Jenny kneels down beside me, and I feel her giving the sleeping back a gentle hug as she says, "I'm sorry, Darla. I wish there was something we could do."

I let out a bit of a muted scream, and Jenny reacts by squeezing a little tighter. Then we sit there in silence for a few minutes as I decide how to best deal with this situation. *Think, Darla, think!*

I keep going over and over the same things in my mind when, all of a sudden, my dad's voice echoes in my head. "*Darlin, just remember you are a Towns.*" Yeah, I need to snap out of this. How bad can it be?

I slowly start to unzip the sleeping bag as Jenny retreats over to hers.

I surface from my cocoon, look over at her, and say, "I'll be fine. This will be fine. I mean, we can still hang out a ton. This is probably just a split for activities or something. It might not be a big deal at all. The only *really* annoying thing is having to listen to Jill's goofy brother."

Jenny gives a surprised look. "The milkshake guy?"

I nod then shrug. "Yep, that's him. My new fearless leader."

Then it's my turn to be surprised when Jenny starts laughing, and it's the kind of laugh like she hasn't heard anything so funny in her entire life. Between large bursts of laughter, she gets out, "What ... are ... the odds?"

Ha, she's right.

Now we both laugh really hard as we hear someone unzip then see them pop their head into our tent.

"What's so funny?" Taylor asks.

For some reason, this makes us laugh even harder as we yell at Taylor to get out of our tent.

After we calm down a bit, Taylor tells us that Sam went to see if there was any way to get me on our team so we could stick together. I appreciate the effort, but I have already accepted that this is just how it is going to be.

"It's probably not that big of a deal," I tell Taylor. "We can all still hang out plenty, I'm sure. This is just for the activities, right?"

Taylor nods.

"I mean, seeing as you are being led by Sam, and we are being led by Bragg, I feel like your chances of winning literally everything are crazy high. That's annoying, but even with *that boy*, I am going to give all of you a run for your money. Darla Towns doesn't back down from a fight."

Taylor puts his hands up as he backs away, smiling all the way. Then he says, "Okay, well then, let's get ready for the opening ceremony. It starts in fifteen minutes over in the leaders' area."

We mock salute Taylor. Then Jenny says, "Sir, yes, sir!"

As he leaves, we look at each other and pick up where we left off, laughing.

This is basically how I need to approach this entire week. I need to make the best of every situation and not take anything too seriously. This is supposed to be fun, and I am determined to make it so.

Jenny and I straighten up our sleeping bags then grab a quick drink of water before heading out to join the other Blue Hill scouts as we walk over to the opening ceremony. We fall in with everyone else, and the normal scouting rituals are underway before we know it.

I have never really been a big fan of this part of scouting, but the ceremony is just something to endure while we wait to get to the good stuff. For me, the good stuff is anything that results in me getting something, whether it's working toward a badge or, in this case, competing to win some prize or another. Anything that lets me show all these boys what girls can really do is fine by me. They are going to learn to take us seriously, that much I do know.

Tracks

Jon

AS SOON AS I GET BACK to our tent city, I head straight to Marc to break the news. I need to fill in everyone, but Marc is probably not going to take the fact that we aren't on the same team particularly well. After all, we are usually attached at the hip as we go through these outings.

As soon as I unzip our tent, I start with, "Marc, you are not going to believe this!"

Marc is a bit startled by my quick entry and bonks me on the head with his pillow. Then, as if that didn't just happen, he asks, "Believe what?"

I explain to him how the leaders split us up into two teams, wanting to encourage us to get to know each other before school starts.

Marc nods as I speak then says, "So, I'm guessing that you and I got split up, right?"

"How did you know?"

"That's just my luck. Whatever. I'm sure it'll be fine. It definitely makes sense that they want us to get to know the Blue Hill guys."

That triggers the even bigger news to come out.

"Yeah, but the Blue Hill guys actually have two girls in their troop."

"What? Girls? That's ... unexpected!" he exclaims.

We talk it through, actually impressed that Blue Hill has some girls.

As soon as the announcement came out that girls are allowed, we had a couple of girls come to a few of our meetings, too. But, for whatever reason, they decided that it wasn't right for them and never stuck around. I guess it could be that they realized that most of us in the Grinwell troop are pretty much like Marc and me. We aren't chock-full of jocks and popular guys, not that the girls care about that type of thing, specifically. I just mean we are a special kind of group that is into the same things and stick together. Well, that's not what I mean to imply, either. Don't get me wrong; all of our guys are great. Well, most of our guys are, at least. We are more into hanging out online and gaming than playing sports or really doing anything else. We probably aren't the most welcoming bunch, either.

Marc and I agree that is something we need to try to change, and this week is a perfect opportunity. We then decide to meet with the rest of the guys and break the news to them together, stressing how important it is that we be open to meeting everyone and give *all* of them a chance, especially the girls.

I'm not sure we totally convince them, but at least we gave it our best effort. Most of them just shake their heads, kick the dirt, and give us the body language that indicates they don't like this, not one bit. I definitely know what it means when I am looking at a bunch of guys with their arms crossed and scowls on their face. This is going to be an uphill battle, but I know these guys, and I'm almost certain they will eventually come around.

After getting that out of the way, Marc and I decide that we better make the best use of our downtime, so we take a quick hike through the woods. We didn't grab Grandpa this time. He was in a deep conversation with the other leaders when we checked on him. We have no idea what they were talking about, but we know better than to interrupt our elders like that. So, off we go into the woods ...

After we get about fifty feet into the trail, Marc notices some footprints heading off the track and into a section of wider trees. The grass is tall and thick, making it hard, if not impossible, to follow wherever this person was going. So, we stop, and I decide to use one of the rhymes Grandpa taught me to do some tracking.

"May these tracks be made abundantly clear
As we try to find the person that must still be near.
Even though this grass is long and way too thick,
May its blades be parted and help us find him real quick."

With that, the grass parts as we walk by, and then snaps back as soon as we pass. This is much easier.

We are led deeper and deeper into the woods until, suddenly, the tracks just stop, as if the person disappeared into thin air.

I look at Marc. "Dead end."

He scratches his head. "That's really strange. Where did he go from here? How does that happen?"

Right as he says this, I swear the ground starts shaking, as do the trees around us, catching both of us by surprise.

We look at each other then all around us.

"What ...? W-what ... was that?" Marc asks with a little bit of fear in his voice.

I shrug. "No idea, but we'll have to come back to this, because we need to get back to camp before we miss the opening ceremony."

Marc agrees, and then we head in the reverse direction as we trace the tracks now backward to where we first uncovered them. I have to admit that is a pretty handy rhyme, even if we didn't find whoever it was who made them. I also want to get back to ask Grandpa and the others if they heard or felt anything.

Was that an earthquake? In Iowa? That just doesn't happen. It was strange and has me feeling nervous with a noticeable pit in my stomach. I can't shake the feeling of being watched. Something is off, really off, and I don't like it.

Ceremony

Darla

OUR TROOP IS LINED up on one side, and the Grinwell troop is lined up with that goofball Jon Bragg in front. We feel the stares of every single scout from Grinwell fall directly on us.

When Jenny and I first started going to scout meetings at Blue Hill, we had the same thing happen, so this is no surprise and doesn't bother us even a little bit. It took a few meetings before everyone at Blue Hill got used to it, but now we are treated just like any other scout. I guess we will have to go through a bit of that again, but I'm sure Sam and Taylor will have our backs. That should help quite a bit, because nobody wants to cross Sam. He is a good head taller than most of the guys here and is about twice as wide. When you're around someone so much, sometimes you forget that. He's like the big brother I never had, and I feel the same way about Taylor. They are good guys, good friends.

The first thing that happens is the presentation of the colors. We stand at attention while a trumpet plays and the flags are presented. When that is completed, we all salute as we say the Pledge of Allegiance. Then the leader tells us to go to the rest position. I just watch Sam and do what he does.

The leader does roll call for each of the troops. Blue Hill is Troop 394, and Grinwell is Troop 107, all scouts are present and accounted for.

Now the leader steps to the front and addresses us. "Welcome to Harmony Grove. This is a special camp since our two troops will be going to school together in the fall. As you have already heard, we will be combining the units into two mixed teams for our activities. Normally, we would compete against each other. We hope that you will do your best to demonstrate the traits of good scouts and welcome each other in the spirit of good sportsmanship and fun."

He goes on for a while and, to be honest, I zone out a little until I hear what is music to my ears.

"We will start with our first activity in fifteen minutes, in the game field over by the mess hall."

Yes! Let's go!

We all run back to our tents to get ready for a competition.

As soon as we all collect on the game field, we are still split up in our troops since that's just natural for us.

"Okay, let's have the Senior Patrol Leaders up here," the leader calls out.

Sam and Bragg get announced, and we are told to line up behind each of them as the names for each team gets called off, as if we don't already know which team we are on.

When my name is called, I walk over to Bragg and glare at him, shaking my head. I still cannot believe this guy is going to be leading our team.

He just flashes a big smile and says, "Hi, Darla. Good to have you on our team."

I'm not sure if that was genuine or not, but he fooled me if it wasn't. At least he seems unfazed by having a "girl" on his team. The rest of the team ... seems a little less than thrilled about it. Let's just say they are giving me plenty of space. *Ha*, fine by me.

We find out the first activity is going to be a potato sack race with all of us pairing up. I have never seen boys scatter away from me so fast. I notice the same thing happening to Jenny, but Sam is already making his way over to her.

I silently thank Sam as Bragg steps over to me and says, "Looks like we're partners. What do you say, Darla?"

I mean, there are literally no other choices, so I simply throw up my hands and nod.

With our history, I just hope he doesn't cause any injuries. I say that, knowing for a fact that I am going to do everything I can do to make sure we win every single event that we do together. I don't know any other way than to go as hard as I can. For me, there is no option but to win. Even if I have to drag Bragg over the finish line, this is going to happen.

We find out that there will be two races in this event. The group is too big to all run at the same time so half of us will go first. The fastest duo from each group will face off against each other in a final race. We are in the second group, so we watch the group before us go.

Jenny and Sam are in that group, along with Taylor and Jon's friend, who have paired up. Sam would probably be better off carrying Jenny than running this race with her. He's so big, and she is super short in comparison. This is not her thing, and so they fall pretty much right after the race starts. Taylor and Jon's buddy are actually pretty good, and they end up winning their round. For some reason, that surprises me. They were actually fast, winning by at least two lengths over the next closest team. I am going to have my hands full beating them with Bragg strapped to me.

Three Legs

Jon

WELL, I HAVE TO ADMIT I was really hoping that the Darla on the list was not *the* Darla, but no such luck. I mean, of course it's her. What are the odds there is another girl named Darla from Blue Hill? The answer is not high.

As she walks over to join my team, I catch a decidedly unhappy glare and just have to flash her the best smile I can muster.

We are going to have to find a way to make the best of this situation. I am positive that I'm the last person on earth that Darla wants to see, and she made that abundantly clear through Jill already. I will have to do my best turn that around. In fact, this is a great opportunity to reset and establish a good rapport with her. After all, she is good friends with Jess, too, so it's likely we will be running into each other on a frequent basis. I wouldn't want her dislike to rub off onto Jess.

The first event is one that Sam selected—the three-legged race using potato sacks. Basically, everyone pairs up, and then each person puts one leg in the burlap bag and both hold onto the bag while trying to run as fast as possible, together, to the other end of the field. At first glance, this doesn't seem like my type of race.

Everyone has paired up, leaving me with just one scout to choose from—Darla, who reluctantly accepts the situation.

C'mon, Bragg, turn on the charm, or at least turn off the clumsy awkwardness so this girl stops hating you.

Fortunately, the Blue Hill teams go first and, to my surprise, Marc and his partner end up winning, with Sam, the giant, falling down pretty quickly, as he is partnered up with the other girl. Somehow, I don't think Darla is going to let me off the hook that easy.

As soon as we line up, Darla turns to me and says, "Don't mess this up, okay? I'll drag your butt if I have to!"

I look her straight in the eye and say, "No pressure then."

Oh, I think she smiled just a little bit there for a split-second, but then she goes straight back into competition beast mode.

We start off, and I do my best to keep up, but we are clearly out of sync. That's when I realize someone has to take the lead and that clearly is going to be her. So, I follow her lead, and we fall into a smooth rhythm. We aren't flying, but we are moving steadily.

We have just one team in front of us as we approach the finish line, and that's when Darla yells, "Dive!"

I do exactly as I'm told, and we barely squeak out a victory. This makes Darla smile.

"Good call on the dive," I tell her.

"I know, right?" Then she's off to go talk with her friends.

I think that's the first time I have ever won anything physical, at least in front of a crowd.

My troop is pumped for me. I mean, us.

Of course, I'm capable of a lot more than that, and I'm not super excited about really winning anything for fear that someone will suspect or uncover my secret.

As we get lined up for the final race, Marc introduces me to his partner for the race, Taylor. We saw them run, and I think they were considerably faster than us, so this should be a foregone conclusion. Darla, apparently, doesn't share this opinion. She comes over with a new plan on how we are going to manage the run, wanting us to practice. I guess I am fine with that. We can move more quickly if I can keep up with her. She is really fast.

They line us up, and then we set off as quickly as possible. Both teams are neck and neck as we make our way down the field. This could be anyone's race. We pull ahead a little, then they pull ahead a little, and it goes on like that for what seems like forever. When we get to the other side, they start to pull away a little, and I start to anticipate the dive. Without Darla having to say anything, I go for it, diving as fast as I can, which brings her crashing down, as well, since she wasn't expecting that. We fall just short of the finish line as Taylor and Marc cross over it.

Darla glares at me. "What was that?"

I shrug. "I thought the plan was to dive at the end again."

"Yeah, it was, but when we actually *got* to the end, not before."

Yeah, that's fair.

"I'm sorry, Darla."

She's super irritated, storming off while saying, "I don't need your apologies, Bragg. I need you to stop messing up so we can win!"

If we keep getting paired up for events, this is going to be a long, long week. At least I didn't rip anything, spill anything, or break anything this time. That's an improvement. Even with that, I think she is now even more angry with me than when we started, which is saying quite a lot.

I head over to congratulate Marc and Taylor and, when I get there, Taylor says, "Don't worry about Darla. She'll get over it."

"Really?"

Taylor shakes his head. "No, not really, but she might be less angry over time."

We all laugh at that.

I certainly seem to know how to press her buttons, whether it's intentional or not.

First Aid

Darla

AFTER LOSING THE THREE-legged race because of *that* boy, I need some time to myself to calm down. There is just something about losing that infuriates me. I know it's not a good thing. I think it's fine to be competitive, but I know I shouldn't be *so* competitive that I can't control my temper. It's been something I have battled all my life. Lately, though, it has only intensified. I just cannot deal. In fact, the more I think about trying to deal with it, the angrier I get, so I'm not really sure how I'm going to break out of this cycle.

After I pound my feet into the ground, leaving deep marks with every step I take, I find myself approaching our tent. I head inside and into the comfort where I can let out some of this emotion without anyone seeing me.

I hear Sam and Jenny arrive outside, but they know me well.

I hear Jenny say, "I think Darla needs a minute." Then I hear them walk away.

Honestly, I probably need a lot more than a minute.

I decide to crack open my scout handbook so I can read ahead a bit about our first activity. If I'm going to make something out of this day, I need to know enough to be sure to qualify for a badge or two by the time this week is over.

Jenny and I have some catching up to do, so we are going to try to make that happen here at the camp. I guess it used to be controversial to earn merit badges at camps versus in a more controlled setting with the troop, but since we are still in our troops, that isn't a problem.

I study page 106 and 110 of the handbook plus a handout Sam gave me that covers the first-aid requirements for all levels. That's one badge that I am targeting for this week. It should be a fairly easy one to get, and it is a required badge, anyway, if I eventually want to be an Eagle Scout. I think it would be a great achievement to be a girl Eagle Scout. Thankfully, this is helping to calm me down as I set my eyes on a bigger prize. Race? What race? That's ancient history.

After calming down, I catch up with Jenny, and we head over to our first activity, which is related to first aid. As soon as I get there, I see that they have the same pamphlet I was reviewing earlier available for everyone.

The first thing we are going to go through is to detail everything that should be in our first-aid kits with an explanation of why we need each item. Of course, pretty much everything in a first-aid kit is self-explanatory, so this isn't going to be super informative.

Apparently, this merit badge normally takes three days to get through all of the requirements. There are just some aspects of the training that must be done whether they are truly helpful to anyone or not. I guess the thinking is that it *could* be helpful.

As we get toward the end of the session, they start talking about first-aid specifically as it applies to being in the woods. This included things like what to do if you think a tick might have landed on your head and things like that. Great, I'm for sure going to think that there are ticks all over my skull now. Why is it that, when someone says anything like that, that body part suddenly becomes extra sensitive?

The leader for this session is old, really old, possibly prehistoric. He has a gray beard that he loves to stroke and is also one of those people lately who rubs me the wrong way. I don't like him, though he seems to be the nicest grandpa type in the whole world. Literally everyone else seems to think he's fantastic, including Jenny. I don't see it, not at all. He seems to take an interest in me, and that's when I realize where I have seen him before. This is Jill's grandpa, which means he is Bragg's grandpa. Yeah, apparently, I just can't get away from that family lately.

Grandpa is showing us how to properly bandage a deep cut and using me as his medical dummy. As he is cutting the tape, the scissors slip, and he cuts my leg. Geesh, what is the deal with the guys in this family?

He immediately applies pressure and tells me to do the same. The bleeding stops quickly, but I have had about enough of first-aid for the day.

He continues to apologize, saying he doesn't know what has gotten into him, getting old, arthritis, etc. I am totally tuning him out at this point.

I head over to the leaders to get tended to, and I'm sure there are some forms that need to be filled out or something really fun like that.

Yeah, this has been quite the first day. I can't wait to see what happens next. Actually no, I can wait. Never mind.

I decide that I'm just going to go back to my tent and lay down for a bit until it is time to eat. With the bleeding stopped and all kinds of things rattling around in my head, it's surprising that I can even think about taking a nap. Before I know it, though, I'm asleep and back at the school in my dreams. Yeah, that sounds about right.

What's weird is I'm aware of the fact that I'm dreaming right now. Is that weird, or is it normal? Do other people know when they are dreaming? I'll have to remember to ask someone, if I don't forget after waking up.

Great. Now I'm distracted by reality when I am dreaming. I don't remember feeling this way before, but maybe I just forget it every time I wake up. I wonder if that's true. I wonder if I'm ever going to stop asking myself questions. Hmm ... maybe.

Leave No Trace

Jon

AFTER THE RACE FIASCO, I'm more than happy to meet up with Marc so we can go to our first activity of the week. We are working on several badges, including our hiking badge, which sounds easy, but there are several hikes required in order to knock this one out and, well, we aren't always in an area where we can hike easily for ten, fifteen, or twenty miles. It's doubtful we will be able to get all of those hikes in this week, but we should be able to make a healthy dent in them, especially given that we have to do some extra hikes with Grandpa. Of course, we will leave the Bragi stuff out of the plans that we turn into our troop leaders and just focus on the hiking relevant parts we intend. It's still a great opportunity to kill two birds with one stone.

Our activity leader is taking us through the best way to plan a hike and the documentation that we should be prepared to turn in to meet the merit badge requirements. I feel like we have this covered, but it's good to make sure. The hiking merit badge is part of an optional set of badges to get Eagle Scout. We could have also chosen the cycling or swimming badges, but this one coincides nicely with other things we need to do, so we are going to at least attempt it. If, for some reason, we just cannot complete the hikes, then we will switch to the swimming or cycling.

The leader is also carefully explaining things we could be looking for here at Harmony Grove. It's a state park, so there is quite a bit of wildlife present, and some of it is specific to the area. We will certainly see a lot of deer if we haven't already, and that is true. After coming to

Harmony Grove several times, I'm surprised we haven't already come across a herd. The biggest predator is a coyote. They can look harmless, but they are far from it. They are not to be messed around with in any way, shape, or form. Duly noted. He talks about the best way to preserve any area that we have been walking in and to make sure that we do our best to have the least impact as possible on the natural environment.

Marc whispers over to me, "This is so boring. I'm not sure how much more I can take."

I quickly respond, "It's certainly not exciting and not really new information, but it is important. We need to know what to be watching for, and it might also help explain the various things we see while hiking. You know, it will help us be prepared."

Both of us smile a little. That's something we like to work into our scouting conversations whenever possible. Everyone knows that a good scout is always prepared. In fact, we use this in almost every situation, from homework to bringing along a lunch if we are doing a mowing job. It's appropriate in so many scenarios. It would be even funnier if it wasn't so accurate.

Just then, someone taps on my shoulder, and I turn around to see Sam, the giant, behind me.

"Hey, Jon, do you two want to plan a hike with Taylor and I?"

"Oh, we would love to do that, but we already have quite a few planned with my grandpa. He's one of the leaders at the camp and has quite a few things he wants to show us." That was probably a mistake to say, because the obvious response comes back from Sam.

"Oh, that sounds interesting. Maybe Taylor and I can tag along with all of you."

While I know for a fact that this isn't possible, I decide to say, "Let me talk with my grandpa and see what he says. I don't really know what is required and/or what other provisions we might need if more people come along.

"Understood, let us know. We're interested."

"Will do," I tell him.

That Sam is all right. He seems like "good people," something my family says when they think someone is down to earth and an all-around pleasant person. Even if he is a giant, he's a friendly giant. I really wish he would put in a good word for me with Darla. It couldn't hurt.

I'm more and more concerned that she is going to further drive Jess away from me, and that is just not okay. I have to figure out a way to head this off. Maybe I'll get lucky, and the next competition will be easier and something that I am more of a natural at doing, or maybe I am going to need a little magical help.

No, I can't use my powers that way. I know better.

I'm actually a little disappointed in myself that the thought crossed my mind. That type of thinking is exactly what got the Loki line in trouble. They wanted to use their powers for their own gain instead of to protect people and to make the world a better place. It's so easy to fall into that trap.

This is not a big deal at all. In the grand scheme of things, whether Darla thinks I'm a worthless, clumsy clown is completely unimportant. This too shall pass. At some point, she will get over it, and if not, then I can just stick with the plan of avoiding her as soon as this camp is over. It's going to be fine.

Circle Up

Darla

I HEAR THE BELL RING again, and then I realize that someone is shaking me.

"I'm up already, Mother!"

That is met by laughter from not my mother, but Jenny, and it sounds like Sam and Taylor, too. Oh boy! Yep, they are all in the tent right now.

"What's going on?" I ask.

"It's time to head over to the mess hall to eat lunch. How is your leg? Do you need any help?" Sam asks.

I look down at my leg that seems completely fine. "I guess not. It must have not been very deep since it looks okay right now."

They all head out the zipper door, and as he is about to leave, Sam does his best Mom impression as he says, "You better get a move on. Our lunch is getting cold!" He laughs as he steps out, and I do exactly that.

I move as quickly as I can as, at about the same exact moment, I realize that I am starving. I mean, I am really, *really* hungry right now.

I catch up with the group before they get to the dining hall—a log cabin with a big old dog sitting on the front porch, along with a whole mess of boys pushing and shoving trying to get to the front of the line. Maybe that is why they call it a mess hall—getting into it sure looks like a mess.

Just about everyone greets Sam, but Jenny and I still get the "girl" stares and off-putting looks.

As soon as they open the doors, the flood of boys comes rushing through and start filling up all the tables that are remotely close to the front of the room and nearest to the kitchen. Our group heads straight to the back as we follow Sam, who is looking for someone. Of course, it is Bragg and his sidekick.

We gather around the table.

I am still a little annoyed by the loss at the race earlier today, so I give Bragg the evil eye. I can't believe he dove early. What was he thinking?

Skipper gets up to say a few words before we eat.

"Okay, you need to have at least one-third of your table from the other troop. So, if you have one hundred percent Blue Hill or one hundred percent Grinwell scouts, mix it up."

There are some significant moans as people reluctantly switch tables, and we hear the screech of sliding folding chairs in unison. It's like every table has a pecking order and the ones at the bottom seem to know it as they are the switchers. I guess we got "lucky" since our table is okay and none of us need to move.

After the noise dies down, Skipper starts back up. "Before we eat, let's all go around the table and answer these questions: Why did you become a scout and what do you want to get out of this week?"

Jenny and I give each other a solid eyeroll, and we are not the only ones. I think this is about the last thing any of us really wants to do, but we want to eat more than we want to fight the task at hand.

Sam starts us off by saying, "I became a scout because I thought it looked like fun, and that's exactly what I want to get out of this week—fun."

Okay, so as you might expect, Taylor greatly approves of this statement. So much so that he decides his answers are exactly the same and just goes with a "Ditto." Nobody is ever going to accuse Taylor of having an independent thought when Sam is around.

I go next and say, "I became a scout because my dad and grandpa were both Eagle Scouts. So, as soon as girls were allowed, I wanted to join to honor that tradition. This week, I just hope to get accepted by everyone."

That gets a reaction from the table, and finally Bragg says, "We are glad you are here. It's pretty cool that both of you stuck it out and want to be scouts."

Okay, that was actually nice of him.

I reluctantly nod and give him a slight smile. It's honestly nice to hear anyone say that.

Jenny is up next. "I joined Scouts because Darla is my best friend, and I didn't want her to go through it alone."

I'm even surprised by that, but I mouth a "*Thank you*" to her.

Then she turns to look at Sam, "And I also want to have fun this week."

Everyone laughs as we all want to lighten the mood a bit.

Bragg says, "I became a scout for a similar reason to Darla. This was something that my dad and I could do together that we both enjoyed. He normally comes as a leader but, since my grandpa is staying with us, my dad said he could come this time instead. Oh, and this week I want to progress toward at least one merit badge on *my* way to Eagle Scouts."

Interesting. The goofball is on a mission, as well.

His friend's name is apparently Marc, who says he joined Scouts to keep Bragg in line, and this week he hopes to help him make some more progress toward their goals, whatever that means. He's surprisingly vague about it.

With that, we are through with the requirements before heading to eat, and none of us have to be told. Within five seconds of Marc finishing, or maybe before he finished, we are all on our feet and walking toward the serving line to get our meals.

Lunch is tacos, I think. It's a little hard to identify the meat that is sitting in the metal serving tray, but it smells like Mexican food, and there are tortillas sitting next to it. They give us each two tortillas, and then one scoop of the mystery meat gets plopped onto each. We then get a scoop of corn, some pears, and a big fried cinnamon stick that looks really tasty. Lunch is served.

Oh Deer

Jon

AFTER LUNCH, IT'S FINALLY time for a bit of Bragi training. Grandpa, Marc, and I head out for a hike. I'm sure Grandpa used the old "Have to walk off my lunch" excuse to get away from the other leaders. In general, Grandpa is a moderately healthy guy and does go for daily walks, even at home, so that excuse makes sense. He even has one of those watches that keeps track of the steps he takes, and boy, does he like to tell everyone how far he has walked every day. Also fine by me, even if it is just a number. He's impressive for his age. At least, he is to me.

I feel fortunate that I don't have to worry about Grandpa while we are hiking. His knees, back, and other joints seem to be just fine, and if they aren't, he never complains. I guess that puts him in a unique group of fortunate people. I wonder if that has anything to do with him being a Bragi or at least having Asgardian essence for so long. Yeah, I'll have to ask him about that someday. That could be a part of what he often describes as "good genes." Ha, of course it is. I cannot believe it took me that long to make that connection. What a dork I am sometimes. Maybe Darla is right about that.

"Jon, pay attention," Grandpa says. "What we are looking for are things that seem or feel out of place, or animals that are showing interesting behaviors."

We look for a while and kind of stroll along the trail, making our way farther away from the camp. We see a whole lot of nothing.

Along the way, Grandpa points out various types of plants and an occasionally interesting flower, or even an insect or two. Then I look up in the distance and see something.

"Grandpa, look at those birds over there circling. Are those buzzards?"

Grandpa nods then shakes his head. "That's a kettle of turkey vultures circling their next victim. You can't even imagine how quickly they can pick apart the carcass of a dead animal. It's a sight to see, for sure. Let's go see what they're eyeing."

We head in that direction and pick up the pace some. Its clear Grandpa is feeling some urgency to get there before the birds do their thing.

As we approach, they start to make a bit more noise, and I get the distinct impression that the turkey vultures aren't exactly happy we are here.

We can make out the frame of a deer laying in the field. This deer looks like it has already been slain and even carved up, as there are significant chunks missing.

"This one is clearly dead," Grandpa points out the obvious. "I wonder why the birds are still circling. Maybe whoever killed this little guy just left and they were waiting for them to clear the area before getting their fill."

We get closer and closer to the deer.

"You want to make sure animals like this are actually dead. They could do anything if there is any life at all left in them." Grandpa gives the deer a little nudge with his hiking boot, and nothing happens. Then he bends down to get a good look at the deer's eyes, and they look peaceful. He then looks up at me and says, "Let's see what caused this little guy's demise, Jon. Are you ready to give it another try?"

I nod as I approach the deer to look into his eyes.

"Dear, deer, with those warm and inviting eyes so brown,

Please give me a glimpse of whatever or whomever it was that took you down."

I see flashes of blue, a blade, a man's hand that is guiding the blade into this deer's flesh. I then see the blood come out and feel an intense sense of pain before it all goes away.

I take a few moments to gather my thoughts and to recover before filling in Marc and Grandpa.

"That's interesting," Grandpa says. "Do you think the blade was used to kill the deer or was that just the hunter carving him up to take some meat for his dinner? He clearly carved it specifically and precisely. This person is good with a knife."

I shrug and reply, "I didn't actually see what brought him down, but he was definitely not dead until he was getting carved up, poor thing. He went through a lot of pain as he was dying." I suddenly get angry about that. I wish I could have been here to protect this deer.

Grandpa can tell I'm getting upset as he says, "Okay, Jon, that's enough for now. Good work with that rhyme. Let's spend some time thinking about that more and see if you can remember anything else after you calm down. For now, let's head back so I can tell the leaders that there are definitely hunters out here."

We start to head back, and my mind clears a bit as we go.

Of course, Marc wanted to stay and watch the turkey vultures, but frankly, I could not stomach another minute of looking at that poor deer.

After a few moments of silence, Grandpa says, "When you get a few minutes, I would like to see if you can draw what that blade looked like for me and any other details you can remember. That might be useful in helping the park rangers and others figure out who might have done this."

I nod then ask, "Sure. But how are you going to explain knowing what the blade looked like?"

He smiles. "Leave that to me, grandson. I've done this type of thing more than a few times."

Once again, I feel a bit foolish, but then I realize that, no, this one is valid.

"Okay, but if I'm going to learn how to handle this, as well, I really need to know what you say."

Grandpa thinks about it for a second then says, "Fair point. I'll let you know."

Sometimes, it pays to be a bit curious. Now, what did that blade look like again? Slowly, let's think this through slowly. It was a weird knife, and not just because it was blue. It was a weird shape, too. *Think, think, think.*

The Tournament

Darla

AS LUNCH IS FINISHING up, Sam tells us about the next activity. I'm sure we were already told, but I, for one, didn't commit whatever they said to memory.

Anyway, next up is a two-man canoe race. That's not something I have done much before, so I ask Sam if we can go down to the water to practice some.

"Sure," Sam says. "Let's all get in our lake clothes then meet up over by the canoes. Sound good?"

Absolutely!

Jenny and I head back to get ready, and she asks, "Have you ever canoed before? Is that even a word? Canoed?"

I laugh and shrug as I say, "I have no earthly idea, but however you say it, yes, I have a few times with my parents, but nothing competitive, so this should be a good challenge."

Jenny turns up her nose a bit. "I don't know. I don't think I'm going to like this one much. I feel sorry for whoever my partner is, and that probably means Sam."

"I would be surprised if Sam couldn't win all by himself."

Jenny agrees and, with that, we switch into one-piece swimsuits, Nike shorts, and dry, fit T-shirts.

As soon as we get to the water, we start digging to find life jackets that will fit us. Sam talks about how to make sure the vest is tight enough to keep us afloat if the boat should flip over, which better not happen. It's snug and slightly uncomfortable, but I would rather be safe than sorry.

Next up, getting into the water. It's surprisingly awkward just to get the canoes in the water then climb in.

As I go to step into it, the canoe slides away, and I'm headed for the splits, when Sam pulls the boat back in and says, "Sorry, I forgot this was new-ish to you."

"No big deal. Fortunately, dance does come in handy sometimes."

He smiles. "Okay, so a couple of things to know about partner canoeing is that the person in the back of the boat is the one that will be steering the boat. The front of the boat is traveling largely in a straight line, cutting through the water. So, I would recommend the most experienced person in the back, or stern, of the canoe."

I nod. "Got it. Don't get into the back. Check."

He laughs. "Probably a good call. Also, it's a bit easier to canoe on your knees instead of sitting down so you can engage your core better." He demonstrates for me, and I basically mimic what he is doing with occasional glances over my shoulder.

Jenny and Taylor are also practicing, so I can watch Taylor, as well. Jenny, not so much. She is having a rough go at it, to say the least.

It takes about half an hour, but I am finally getting into a good groove with Sam. I think I understand how this works well enough.

Sam says, "You are doing great. You really are a fast learner."

I respond with, "As long as I have a good teacher, I can usually pick things up quickly."

He then looks over at Taylor and says, "Jenny, on the other hand ... not so much."

I have to giggle a little. They have tipped over their canoe probably a dozen times. I have to give Taylor credit for having a ton of patience with Jenny.

I look over and offer some encouragement, "Hang in there, Jenny. You'll get the hang of it!"

Jenny shakes her head. "Nah, I'm good. Let's take a break."

Recognizing that this is probably a good idea, we head back to the dock where several scouts have already gathered for the canoe races. They have everything that was stacked up thrown into the water—canoes, kayaks, paddle boats, and paddle boards. I didn't realize so many of us were in the water.

Skipper calls us all back to land and lays out the rules of the race. It's similar in that the teams will race amongst themselves to find the quickest duo, and then that duo will race head-to-head to determine the overall winners.

Everyone pairs up again and, to nobody's surprise, they are the same pairings. Jenny and I are left to our own, which means I get Bragg and she gets Sam. She is so lucky to be his partner. He is awesome!

I look over and say, "Okay, Bragg, I assume you have done this before, so Sam says you should be in the back, and I'll take the front. Sound good?"

"Sure, whatever you say, boss! I don't mind the bow or the stern, to be honest. And yes, I have done this many times."

Well, that's encouraging. If he has some experience, maybe this is the one thing that he isn't terrible at. We shall see.

We check the bracket to see who we will be racing first then wait our turn.

Several rounds go by, and we actually aren't terrible together. Bragg and I have won every race and, as I predicted, Sam is pretty much winning for Jenny, as well. I'm not sure if she is doing anything much to help, but she is definitely not falling into the water, so that's a big improvement.

We watch as Sam and Jenny defeat Marc and Taylor, and the look on Taylor's face is priceless. He cannot believe it, but I also imagine he wishes Sam was his partner and not Jenny.

Bragg and I also manage somehow to win, so it will be us versus Sam and Jenny for the final.

Before the race, I decide to say, "Can we just try to win this one, please? Just for the record, there is no diving or anything like that before the finish line."

"Hardy har, har, very funny. I didn't mean to lose, you know. I really am sorry about that."

I look him square in the eyes and say, "Well, we did, and I don't want to make a habit of it. Got it?"

He backs away with his hands up. I guess I made my point.

As we hit the water for the final time, Sam and Bragg wish each other luck, and I do the same with Jenny. I am so proud of her, even if Sam is carrying them. I want her to do well, just not as well as me.

The race starts, and we are cruising along a good couple boat lengths in front of Sam and Jenny. It looks like Bragg is finally not going to let me down. However, just as we get close to the finish, the boat rocks hard, and I feel movement in the back. As I turn to look, I see Bragg standing up, and then the boat flips over.

Ugh! This water is gross!

I grab for the canoe as Sam and Jenny go sailing by onto victory.

I look over at Bragg as we hold onto the canoe, still in the water, and ask, "What was *that* all about?"

Bragg won't even look at me as his face turns all kinds of colors. "I thought I saw someone in the woods, watching us. I couldn't tell who it was for sure, but after I stood up, they ran off really fast. I lost sight of them then lost my balance."

I am spitting mad. "*Keep your head in the game, Bragg*!"

I don't even wait for him; I just swim back to shore.

When I get there, Jenny is about as excited as she has ever been. Her happiness is impressive, even though I'm mad at Bragg. I am happy for her and Sam.

Focus, Darla, be happy for your friends.

Ugh! That boy is driving me crazy!

The Blade

Jon

I KNOW DARLA IS MAD, but that just isn't important right now. I don't care about any race. I need to talk to Grandpa and Marc.

As soon as I find Marc, he says, "You could have won! Why did you stand up?"

I look him dead in the eye and say, "It doesn't matter. We need to find Grandpa fast!" With that, I am off to where the leaders are as quickly as I can run, which is to say I am sprinting but holding back so it isn't too fast to be normal.

Marc is hot on my heels.

As soon as we reach him, I see that he is sitting in his lawn chair with an umbrella over his head, catching a nap. I startle him with, "Grandpa! Grandpa!" I would have said more, but I needed to catch my breath for a minute, and he is still getting his bearings, anyway, from getting woken up.

"What in the world is all the ruckus about?" Grandpa asks. "Can't a man get a couple minutes of shut eye?" As soon as he looks into my eyes, though, he asks, "What happened?"

By that time, I have caught my breath and am ready to spill it. I think about saying it slowly, but there is no good way to say what is probably the craziest thing I have ever said. "I saw Coach Locke!"

Marc gasps, and Grandpa just raises his eyebrows and scratches his beard.

Marc has a look of terror on his face as he asks, "What? We—I mean, you—*killed* him, right? How is that possible?"

I wish I knew, but I don't. All I can say is, "Yeah ... I thought I did at least."

"Okay tell me everything," Grandpa instructs.

I explain all about the canoe races and that, in the last race, as we were winning, and I saw something move in the woods by the lake. At first, I thought it was some sort of hallucination or something, so I shook my head then stopped what I was doing to stand up and take a better look. Sure enough, I saw him again. As soon as he saw me and we made eye contact, he took off running and fast, really fast. He was gone in an instant. I go on to say that I have no idea how long he was there or what he was doing, but I'm positive that it was him and not a daydream or any other type of vision. It *was* him.

Marc is looking more and more uncomfortable by the second, and I don't blame him after what Coach Locke put him through, but calming him down is going to have to come secondary. Right now, we have to figure this out.

"I'm not saying I do or don't believe you, Jon," Grandpa says, "but can you do something for me first?" When I nod, he says, "Can you draw that blade you saw from the deer's eyes for me?" Grandpa pulls out some paper from the backpack that he has by his side.

I nod and begin to draw. I have thought long and hard about this, so it is crystal clear in my mind right now. As soon as I get from the tip to the handle, I can see a spark of recognition in his eyes.

He looks up at me and says, "It's a Laevateinn! I don't believe it! How did he ...?" He turns and starts pacing, deep in thought. Then he turns back to us. "That's the sword that Loki used to slay a rooster named Víðópnir. It is said to be magical, but I do wonder why you saw it as blue. This is interesting indeed. I'll need to talk to the APS about this and see if they have heard about any Loki appearances. I also want to know exactly what they found when they cleaned out Locke's place after that blood rhyme." Then, as he turns to go, he says, "Be careful, boys. If this is Coach Locke as Loki, he is most definitely going to be looking for revenge. Keep a sharp eye out for anything unusual."

Marc and I both nod, understanding the seriousness of the situation, then Grandpa heads off to call the APS.

I turn to Marc. "Are you okay?"

He shakes his head. "No, not okay. I am definitely not okay. Coach Locke was a monster, and that was before what we did to him and Dustin! How did he survive that?"

"I have no idea. Maybe I did something wrong, or he somehow outsmarted me. Loki is tricky like that. Maybe he was super charged with a ton of blue essence. It could be anything with that son of a giant! We both know that for a fact from what we've read."

Marc nods but says, "Yeah, but we heard the pops when he and Dustin were torn apart by the blood rhyme. It was a noise I will never forget, for sure."

Of course, I know that sound well. It has haunted me since the day I used the blood rhyme. Part of me, though, is relieved, because if he is alive, then I didn't really kill him and maybe I'm not responsible for any deaths after all.

It's not that he didn't deserve it, but I still feel so guilty for what I did. That had to be horrible to experience. Obviously, it would have been fast but extremely painful.

What I don't understand is, if it is indeed Coach Locke, why has he not made a move yet? What is he waiting for? What is he planning?

I suddenly realize that this week has changed in an instant. It's no longer a fun getaway with the boys, or even with the girls. This changes everything.

Marc and I head back to the tent in stunned silence, both deep in thought. It's doubtful that either of us is going to get much sleep this week, knowing what we now know.

The other thing that is gnawing at me is whether or not we say something to Skipper or to the other scouts. I mean, we all could be in serious danger. Then again, Coach Locke seemed to be intent on just finding and harming Asgardians before, so it could be just me who is in danger. I guess I'm okay with that. It's better than the alternative of my whole troop and the Blue Hill troop having to worry. Of course, Coach Locke knows the best way to get to me now is through my friends, so I need to keep a really close eye on them. Marc and Grandpa may be in even more danger than I am, depending upon whether or not he is powered up on blue essence or not.

Maybe that's why he hasn't attacked—does he have any blue essence left? Somehow, I feel like I'm going to find out soon. Too soon. I need to anticipate something unexpected for sure.

No Way

Darla

AS SOON AS JENNY GETS back, she is literally about as excited as I have ever seen her. Even though we all know Sam carried her through to the win she still didn't make any big mistakes ... unlike the someone *I* was working with. With teamwork, that is super important.

Jenny turns and says, "I'm sorry, Darla. I know you would have won if Jon didn't stand up like that. Why did he do that?"

I let out a sigh. "I don't know. His excuse was he saw something or someone, and that distracted him." I throw my arms up, not really knowing what else to say.

"You know, I don't think I have ever won anything before. I know I didn't really do much, but it still feels pretty awesome. I get why you love winning! I just feel badly that it wasn't you." She lowers her head.

I shake my head. "No, seriously, you guys won fair and square, and don't say you didn't do anything; you did exactly what Sam asked you to do, didn't you?"

She lifts her head as she says, "Yeah, I guess I did."

"There you go. You did great! Congratulations!" I give her a big hug, and that releases all the tension in the tent. I'm kind of glad she won, I'm happy for her and content with sharing this moment with her.

Jenny giggles a little. "Bragg sure has a way of making your life difficult, doesn't he?"

"Tell me about it! That boy is so frustrating. I don't know how Jess puts up with him."

Jenny laughs a little louder. "Well, everyone loves to be adored, right? Clearly, Jon has a thing for Jess. I could tell that after just seeing them at the bowling alley. He was all googly-eyed around her."

I didn't even think of that. I was so preoccupied with just avoiding him and all the accidents that I never realized that he does actually act the goofiest around Jess.

"Yeah, you're right. That totally makes sense. I wonder what the deal is with those two. Did they ever date, or has he always just been like this?"

"Taylor can probably ask Marc, if you want to find out," Jenny says.

"Nah, it's not important enough to involve anyone else."

"Good, for a second there, I thought maybe you were into Jon."

I slug her in the arm. I don't normally do that, but that certainly deserved a solid response. "Shut up! I did *not* say that!"

She unconvincingly replies, "Sure, whatever."

I have to change the subject, or this is going to ruin my attitude completely. "Let's study some more for the first-aid merit badge. I'd like to try to see if we can earn that one before the week is up."

"Sure. Nice change of subject. Let's study."

We go over the first-aid kit contents again and why each item is important, working our way down the handbook. I know it's probably overkill, but if I'm going to make Eagle Scout, I have a serious amount of catching up to do and cannot miss any opportunities for badges.

With my dad and grandpa being Eagle Scouts, I'm sure it would mean a lot to them if I was able to follow in their footsteps. Plus, Jenny and I could be the first girls in the area to make it all the way through. How cool would that be? Maybe that would encourage other girls to give Scouts a try. It's kind of like wrestling—if I'm given a shot to do something special, I feel a responsibility to take it. That's why I was so excited when everything changed at the Boy Scouts and girls were allowed. I could never really get into the Girl Scouts; it just wasn't the same. Good cookies, though. Too good, at least for us dancers.

I do wonder what my mother thinks of all of this. She is generally not as supportive of things that are outside of "normal." She stresses that over and over. "*Why can't you just behave like a normal, regular girl? Why do you always have to stand out and be special?*" It's not exactly the greatest pep talk if I'm honest. I just don't get her. She is this strong-willed and powerful woman, yet she is super set in her ways and when it comes to her beliefs. There really is just her way, and then the wrong way. She just doesn't have the ability, or desire, to see things from my perspective. I seriously doubt she understands my desire to be an Eagle Scout, but I'll just have to ignore that.

Lately, I have gotten pretty good at ignoring her. What irritates me, though, is she pushes the things she wants me to do so hard, like dancing, but doesn't get it when I show the same passion and dedication to something else. It's beyond frustrating.

Okay, well, whether Dad or Mother are happy about this, I must actually focus and achieve it first. I do really want *both* of them to be proud of me, but I'll settle on one of them if I need to.

In the end, this is something I want to do for me, as well. After all, once an Eagle Scout, always an Eagle Scout. It's one of those rare things that, once you attain it, it is associated with you for life. That means something to me. That is more important than everything I have to go through to earn it all rolled up into one. So, even if I wasn't one of the first girls, or if my dad and grandpa are proud, or whatever Mother thinks, it's all secondary to the goal. Somehow, some way, I will make this happen, even if I have to endure being teamed up with that stupid boy.

Ha, it's so funny that Jenny thinks I like him. Whatever gave her that idea? That's just ridiculous.

The Hike

Jon

AFTER ALL THAT HAPPENED today, I'm really not in the mood to be around anyone. So, after grabbing a quick bite in the mess hall, I decide to snoop around a bit in the woods to see what I can find.

No matter what direction I go, every path just leads to trees and more trees, but no sign of anyone can be found. I wander around for a good hour before giving up and heading back to the tents to try to catch up with Grandpa and Marc.

Grandpa is nowhere to be found, which is odd, but Skipper says that he had to run an errand back in Grinwell. I have a pretty good idea what that's all about. Most likely, he is meeting up with the APS. That is great news. At least then we will get some more information.

With nothing else left to do, I decide to call it an early night, and Marc and I hang out in the tent.

I look over at him and say, "I can't help wondering, if that really was Coach Locke, did Dustin survive, too?"

Marc reacts as if he is thinking the same thing. "I know! At this point, I guess anything is possible. I don't know how, but there are so many things about Asgardians I don't understand that I am open to anything."

I know exactly what he means. I feel the same way.

We don't have much more to say, so we decide to try to drift off into sleep. Fat chance of that, though.

Every noise makes me jump out of my skin and sends me outside to poke around. All I know is this is going to be a long night. Just thinking about the possibility of Coach Locke being out there has me on the highest alert possible. It's concerning. If he is here and is risking being seen by the APS, he can only be thinking about revenge, or he has some other trick up his sleeve that is even worse. If that is possible.

There is something about being up late that brings an incredible amount of paranoia. I'm not sure if everyone feels the same way, or if this is something that is just a personal problem, but my brain is on overdrive right now.

I look over at Marc, who is fast asleep. You would think that he would be the most afraid of the possibility of Coach Locke being back. He might be looking at it logically. The evidence we have up to this point is flimsy at best.

I saw a blade in the eyes of a dead deer that could have possibly been a weapon that the Loki line is associated with, but it could also have been just a hunter's knife. I saw a big man watching us in the canoe race from the shore, but there are lots of really big guys in this area. So, who knows? That could have been a random stranger who was the same stature as Coach Locke. I also know that the blood rhyme that I used on him and Dustin should have been lethal, even to Asgardians/giants like them. Yeah, I need to follow Marc's lead here and try to get some rest. I'm overthinking this.

It's a short night but I have dream after dream of Coach Locke and Dustin. I even dream that I woke up and had a hand over my mouth, as if someone was trying to stop me from speaking. It was a large hand and felt eerily familiar.

When I open my eyes, I am startled to find that Grandpa is staring at me with his nose about two inches away from my face.

"Shh ..." he says. "It's just me, Jon. We need to talk."

When I finally come to my senses and he removes his hand from my mouth, I whisper, "You scared the heck out of me, Grandpa."

He nods. "Sorry about that. Let's take this outside." He points over at Marc then holds a finger up to his mouth to quiet me again.

I just nod and follow him out of the tent.

As soon as we are far enough away from all the tents and down by the water, Grandpa starts, "So, I ran everything by the APS. They haven't heard of anything that would specifically point to a Loki in the area. I didn't tell them about your gift of seeing into the eyes of the dead yet. That is just going to be too tempting for them, and you aren't ready for that. So, some of our proof isn't known to them."

"Maybe you should just let them know."

Grandpa shakes his head. "No way. They would want to use that all the time. We just need to keep a watch out for any more signs of Coach Locke, okay?"

I nod. Of course, I didn't need to be told that. I'm already constantly looking over my shoulder.

By the time we get back to the tents, everyone is already awake and getting ready to head to the mess hall for breakfast. We don't waste too much time in the morning because breakfast is quite good at the camp. The cooks always have a great main dish, like biscuits and gravy, but they also have a line for made-to-order omelets that is insanely popular.

We can't get down there fast enough. I guess we all worked up quite the appetite yesterday and while we were sleeping.

While at breakfast, Skipper tells us the plan for the day. Of course, Sam and I already know the plan. We are going to split up into a few groups and head out for a long hike with various leaders. This time, I make sure that Marc is in my group since we have some more specific exploring to do. We also have Grandpa as one of the leaders, which is going to be helpful, as he can distract the others while Marc and I poke around. We have about fifteen minutes to get ready for the hike and to fill our canteens or water bottles, whatever each scout brought with them. We are going to need it for this long of a hike, along with food and the usual hiking supplies.

As we head out, we have Sam, Taylor, Jenny, and Darla in our group. We all walk together for a while as Grandpa gives out various facts about the trees and plants near the trail.

Marc and I veer off the path for a bit and start to look for any signs of you know who. Then, as I'm starting to say a rhyme, I hear someone following us and turn around to see Darla and Jenny.

"You can finish. Your poetry is interesting. What are you two up to, anyway?"

I look at Marc then back at her. "Marc and I were just looking for things we might have lost out here."

She looks at Jenny then back to us. "Are you looking for the Grinwell High clipboard? Jenny and I saw it out here."

"What?" I ask. "Where did you see it?"

"It's not much farther. We just figured it might be part of a task or something that we would be doing either today or later."

"Can you show us?" I ask.

"Sure, I guess when we get a little farther, but if there is some sort of prize or anything, we call dibs."

"I'm sure there isn't, but deal."

This is interesting. I can hardly wait to get my hands on that clipboard to see if it belongs to who I think it belongs to. Why it would be out here, though, is certainly another mystery to solve.

One of a Kind

Darla

THIS HIKE IS KIND OF boring. We learn about why we need nature trails and things like that. Deep down, I think all of us know it isn't just so we know where we are going. It's as much for the protection of the environment as it is for the safety of us hikers, but I'm not sure it makes for the most interesting conversation. Everyone seems to feel the same way as they all point out different animals and things that they see as we move along.

I notice that Bragg and Marc are lagging and randomly straying off the trail. I wonder what those two are up to. That seems interesting, at least.

I grab Jenny, and we head over to investigate. As we catch up with them, Bragg is whispering some more of his poetry, which is odd, but I have noticed he likes to do that a lot. I may have to ask Jess about that, or possibly his sister. For now, it's strange but also not bad.

Bragg tells us he is looking for something, and I mention the clipboard Jenny and I found. They are super excited about seeing it. So, we head off to where Jenny and I found it.

As we get near the patch of trees and bushes, we see that the clipboard is still right where we left it. Bragg snatches it up. It's quite dirty, more so than what we remember, but we didn't pay that close attention when we first saw it.

Marc says, "This clipboard belonged to Coach Keith. It's a list of wrestlers on the team, ranked by their records. Oddly, though, the names are all crossed off."

They then remind us that Coach Keith was the one who was killed by some animal while he was hunting, but they didn't think it was in Harmony Grove. People aren't supposed to hunt here, so someone must have brought it here for some reason.

"I guess whoever it was felt like they didn't need it anymore," Bragg says.

Jenny and I look at each other and say, "I guess not" in unison.

Unfortunately, it appears as though this clipboard wasn't a part of any activities like we originally thought. It's just here as a result of littering. That's unfortunate.

Marc and Bragg decide they should bring the clipboard back to the scout leaders, so they stick it in their pack, and then we head back to rejoin the hike.

Jenny struggles to keep up, so her and Marc lag behind a bit while Bragg and I take the lead.

I ask Bragg, "Do you mind if I ask you something?"

Bragg shrugs. "Sure. Something about hiking?"

"No, I'm curious about the deal with you and Jess." Bragg coughs, but I continue, "I noticed you seem to like her, and I just wanted to know if there was more to that story. I'm kind of direct, if you haven't noticed, so no sense in beating around the bush."

Bragg clears his throat after choking on that then says, "Um ... Yeah, about that. Jess is great, and I do like her, at least as a friend. We have known each other since forever, but Brad and her are really tight and, of course, they are a perfect match."

I get that. "Yeah, the cheerleader and the quarterback. It's almost too perfect."

Bragg laughs a little. "Yeah, it's something all right."

I can tell he's uncomfortable talking about it, which means Jenny and I are right about this one. That's interesting. I could say something to Jess when I get back, but what is there to say really? Bragg is all right, but he's no QB1. I suppose she is aware of the situation, anyway.

After we walk a bit in silence, Bragg asks, "What about Sam. Are you and Sam a couple?"

I outright laugh at that. "No way. Sam and I are just friends. Great friends, but just friends. Actually, Sam, Taylor, Jenny, and I are all just friends. We hang out a lot at school and share a lot of the same interests, that's all."

"I see. When did you move to Blue Hill?"

I tell him how we moved here this past school year, about our family situation, and how my dad came back to run the family farm. It means a lot to him but is completely different than how our lives used to be in West Des Moines. I tell him how, at first, I hated it, but it has grown on me. It's home now. We then start talking about the schools merging and how weird that's going to be.

Bragg tells me that, like most small towns in Iowa, at one point, our schools were rivals. Then, somehow, the community moved past that and/or the economic reality of it all necessitated the change. I remind him, though, that it will probably be easier for the Grinwell students since we are all going to be in *their* school with *their* teachers. For the Blue Hill students, it will all be new and just like starting over again, which is especially hard on juniors and seniors.

I think we talk for the entire rest of the hike. I learn a lot about his family and how close they are. I tell him that my dad and I are like that, too, but Mother is a whole different story. She is a powerful woman. Bragg thinks that's pretty hilarious and says, "I guess that is where you get that from then, huh?"

I slug him in the arm. "You know, girls don't like to be told they are like their mothers, right?"

"Why not? My parents are great, and it's just an observation. You seem like you are driven and know what you want. It's a compliment, I think, to compare you to your stubborn ... Ah! Got it!"

I laugh, as does Bragg.

Yep, he's still a goof.

Finally, he asks, "Why do you call me Bragg and not Jon?"

Now, that's a good question.

Right about then, the hike is over, and as Jenny and I head back to our tent, I intentionally say, "See you later, Jon. Good talk."

He smiles.

Call Home

Jon

AFTER OUR GROUP HIKE, Grandpa, Marc, and I head to our tent to talk about the clipboard we found. I'm holding onto it, with Marc and Grandpa standing over my shoulders, reading along.

"So, this clearly belonged to Coach Keith, but the question remains: was Coach Keith the last person to use this or Coach Locke?" We all talk about how it's strange that the names on the list are crossed out, almost like a shopping list. All of these wrestlers that haven't graduated are still on the team, so this isn't a list of wrestlers that got cut during tryouts. It's possible that Coach Keith used this as a checklist of sorts to determine whether each wrestler completed a workout, or it's also possible that Coach Locke used this to eliminate the wrestlers from being Asgardians. We naturally jumped to that conclusion, but it's not necessarily the case.

We also don't know Coach Keith's handwriting to know whether or not he even wrote this list. For now, we all agree that it is suspicious at best, and we should turn it over to the APS to take a look at and determine if Coach Locke had this in his possession through fingerprint analysis or whatever methods they use.

Grandpa finishes by saying, "It could be something, or it could be nothing. Either way, we will know soon enough."

Immediately after lunch in the mess hall, it's the designated time for us to call home and talk to our families. Marc and I decide we can wait a bit to make our calls, so we head out to the lake to take a canoe out and just cruise the lake to see if we see any signs of Locke.

When we get to the other side, we see something sticking out of the ground up on a hill. We pull the canoe out of the water and head to take a look.

There are two makeshift grave markers with a talisman hanging from one of them that's really strange-looking. It's a circle with curled lines at the bottom that curve up to meet near the bottom center of the circle. It's like a rollie fingers mustache, but the curls come inward instead of outward. Strange. Clearly, someone put it there on purpose, and it's probably not a good idea to disturb *any* grave, let alone one with an unknown object on it.

We look around, but we don't see any indicators of how long the graves have been here or if anyone has even been around them recently. Striking out on any more clues, we head back to the canoe to cross the lake and make our phone calls home.

As soon as we get back to the other side, I draw the shape of the talisman. Marc agrees that it is a reasonable enough match. This is another thing to run by Grandpa.

At the mess hall, we see the line to call home is significantly shorter now, so we might as well fall in then find Grandpa after our calls.

Marc goes first. It doesn't take long because his mom isn't much of a talker and, unlike my family, they aren't as close. It doesn't really bother Marc. It's just how they are. They love each other; they just aren't ones to spend a lot of time together or really communicate much at all. However, if Marc needs his folks, they are there for him, and vice versa. Plus, Marc has all but been adopted by my family, so he gets plenty of attention from my parents. He really might as well be my brother, which would be fine by me.

When it's my turn, Mom picks up the phone.

"Hi, Jon-boy, how is everything at Harmony Grove?"

"It's pretty much the same as last year. Marc and I are having a good time exploring, and we are even making new friends."

"Oh, that's nice."

"Oh, and I don't know if Grandpa told you, but the troop from Blue Hill is here, as well. They thought it would be a good idea for us to get to know each other, so we are mixing up the troops for activities and while eating at the mess hall."

"Well, isn't that nice of them? And smart, too!" Then she says, "Your father and sister are here to say hello to you."

"Hi, Dad, Jill!" I call out.

Dad jumps in with an overly ambitious, "Hello, son! Miss you! I hope Grandpa is imparting all kinds of wisdom on you guys."

"He is. No worries about that, Dad."

They all think that's funny and laugh.

"Your lawn mowing business is booming!" Dad says. "The Wellington twins are so happy with the job I am doing and say that you are going to have some big shoes to fill when you get back."

"Great, Dad. That's just swell."

He laughs.

"Hey, Jill, guess what?" I say.

She is less than thrilled and doesn't feel like entertaining me, obviously, as she mumbles, "What?"

"There are two girls in the Blue Hill troop."

"Cool."

"One of them is Darla from dance, and her and I have been on the same team for most of the activities."

"*What?*" she yells. "You better not do something clumsy or anything else to tick her off!"

"Actually, we're getting along fine. We just had a great talk on our group hike."

Dad tries to add some positivity, "Well, that's nice, Jon. Way to welcome her to the Scouts!"

"Wait," Jill interrupts. "You were hiking with her? Just her?"

"No, all of us were hiking, but her, Jenny, Marc and I were in a group by ourselves for a bit."

"Do you like her?" Jill asks.

"Yeah, she's all right."

"Is she your new G-I-R-L friend?"

Ah, there it is. Jill in her true nature, giving me a hard time.

I sharply say, "*No*, she's not my G-I-R-L friend. Don't be ridiculous!"

With that, my time is up and so is my patience for this conversation, so I say goodbye then head outside, where I nearly bump into Darla and Jenny, who are standing there with their hands on their hips.

Great. I hope they didn't just hear *all* of that!

Froggy

Darla

AS SOON AS JON WALKS out from making his call, I have to ask, "Who is not your G-I-R-L friend, Jon?"

He turns about as red as a clown nose and stumbles to say, "Um ... How much of that conversation did you hear?"

Jenny and I start laughing.

"Enough, Jon, we heard enough," I reply.

"Jill is always giving me a hard time, so don't take any of that the wrong way."

"What shouldn't I take the wrong way, Jon?" I lean a little bit closer and brush some dirt off his shoulder as he takes an awkward step backward. I realize that I enjoy putting him through this way more than I should.

"It's just that I told Jill we had a good talk on the hike and, of course, she is jumping to conclusions and generally just teasing me a bit. Come to think of it, kind of like you are doing right now, right?"

I smile and bat my eyes. "I have no idea what you mean, Jon."

He smiles as I wind up to give him a good pop on the shoulder with my fist.

"You're all right, Jon Bragg. I may have misjudged you a bit."

Just then, he turns to look into the woods, as if he sees something again. "Will you excuse me, please?" he says then runs off as fast as he can toward the trees.

"Good talk, Jon!" I shout after him.

He's not paying any attention.

"Where is he going?" Jenny asks.

"Who knows? That boy is different."

"Different good, or different bad?" Jenny asks.

"Just ... different."

"Uh-huh, sure, Darla. You keep telling yourself that."

I guess it's time for her to start giving me a hard time. Honestly, I have no idea how I feel about Jon. I mean, he is strange, but not in a bad way exactly.

"Yeah, he is intriguing; that's for sure," I acknowledge.

With that, Jenny lets it drop, and we head back to our tent for a quick snack before we're off to the next first-aid session. I am bound and determined to get that badge this week, no matter what it takes.

When we get back to our tent, we see that our stuff has been moved around. Our sleeping bags aren't where we put them, and our other bags are opened, our belongings scattered, which we most definitely did not do. So, this can only mean one thing.

The boys have either pranked us, or they are hazing us.

Either way, I'm not putting up with this nonsense.

We head to find Sam and Taylor to get to the bottom of this, stat.

We find Sam and Taylor taking a nap in their tent. And that is too much to resist. I think a little bit of payback for them waking me up earlier this week and retribution for the ransacking. What can we do to these boys?

I look at Jenny. "I have an idea."

She grins. "I hope it's about how we're going to get back at them."

I nod. "Most definitely."

As soon as we get outside, I tell her, "We should collect a bunch of the frogs that we've seen hopping all around."

Jenny scrunches up her nose. "That's pretty gross."

But, being from Blue Hill, none of us girls are afraid of getting our hands dirty. We collect a whole bag full of frogs, which sounds like it would take a bunch of time, but they are literally everywhere.

I used to think frogs slept during the day, but obviously nobody told these frogs that, because they are full of all kinds of energy.

Once we have a couple dozen of them, I turn to Jenny and say, "That's enough. Let's go give those boys a little surprise."

We head over and quietly release the frogs into their tent, and then we step back and wait for the reaction. This takes all of about two minutes before we hear a really high-pitched scream, and then we see Taylor running out of the tent.

I guess we know who screamed. Ha!

Jenny and I are laughing hysterically when Taylor sees us and heads right over.

"Not. Funny."

We see Sam then leaving the tent with his arms full of frogs. He releases them. That's not nearly as much fun but also not even a little bit surprising. He wasn't fazed at all. Or, if he was, he isn't letting on.

As soon as he has what he thinks is all of them collected, he casually walks over to us and asks, "Um, what was that all about?"

Jenny looks at me, and I say, "Just a little payback for whatever you boys did to our tent earlier."

"I have no idea what you're talking about," Sam says. "Taylor and I wouldn't mess with you girls; you know that."

Suddenly, I feel like I'm now the one turning different shades of red.

"We're sorry, guys," Jenny tells them. "We thought it was you two."

"No way! Not us," Taylor exclaims. "What exactly happened?"

"Somebody went through our things and moved our sleeping bags around. Basically, nothing seems gone, so we figured it was a prank of some sort," Jenny replies.

"That sounds like a pretty lame prank, doesn't it?" Sam asks.

I guess he's right.

Then Sam says, "I mean, now that we know where your heads are at, I think we can accommodate a little prank war if that's what you want."

I immediately respond, “No, that’s definitely not what we want. We’re sorry.”

“We’ll see about that,” Taylor says. “Sleep peacefully tonight, girls. I’m sure nothing at all is going to happen to your tent.”

Suddenly, I feel like I made a big mistake. No, a *huge* mistake. This is something we are going to regret, no doubt about that.

The Vile

Jon

I RUN OFF SO QUICKLY into the woods that I don't even have time to grab Marc or talk to Grandpa. I could have sworn that I saw Coach Locke watching me back at the mess hall when I was talking to Darla and Jenny. Where is he?

I run around the trails as fast as I can, looking for any sign of him, but I don't see anything. When I come to a fork in the path, I decide it's time to try a rhyme to see if I can save a bit of time.

I drop to my knees and close my eyes.

"Help me get on the right path
So I can see the person I know who was watching me.
A little light is all I need
To illuminate the way and give me some kind of lead."

With that, a burst of sunlight hits the path to the right. I head in that direction. Then I see the sun hit a bunch of bushes and know that I'm going to find something over there.

I leave the path and comb the area, looking for any kind of clue. Sure enough, I find a vile. There isn't anything in it, but I have a pretty good idea exactly what this means. I put it in my pocket then head back to the camp as fast as possible to find Grandpa and Marc.

I know there are training sessions going on, but I have to tell Grandpa about this as fast as possible.

I find Marc first since I knew exactly what he was planning to do, and then I head over to the first-aid training to pull Grandpa out of that.

When we get there, he has just gotten done showing some scouts how to bandage certain wounds. They are deep in the process of practicing, so we pull Grandpa to the side and fill him in on the latest news.

I start first by describing how I saw someone watching me and ran after them. Grandpa frowns, and I immediately know that I shouldn't have run off by myself. That's fine. We can come back to that. Then I pull the vile out of my pocket.

"I found this in the woods."

Grandpa grabs it, smells the inside, and then scratches his head. "This is really strange, boys. I talked with the APS about all of this, and they confirmed that Coach Locke and his boy were deceased when they found them at the house, or what was left of them."

At this point, I am extremely confused, but I ask, "But, what about this vile? That has to be his, right?"

Grandpa shakes his head. "I don't know, Jon. But they were clear on what they did with the remains, so I don't see how this is possibly his, unless it was here a long time ago."

That can't be right.

Completely preoccupied in thought, Marc asks, "What did they say they did with the remains?"

"They are confident that they buried them out in the middle of nowhere where nobody would be, and they even put talismans on the graves. They are certain that those two are gone for good."

As soon as we hear that, Marc looks at me and asks, "Where exactly did they bury them?"

"In a remote area on the other side of the lake, where virtually nobody ever goes," Grandpa answers.

My eyes light up as I say, "Grandpa, I think we saw those graves earlier. We were going to tell you, but then all of this happened, and we didn't get a chance."

"We saw one grave with a cross made out of tree branches and a medallion hanging on it, but—"

"The other grave didn't have anything at all on it, just a cross," I cut Marc off.

Grandpa looks back and forth at us and asks, "What did the talisman look like?"

Marc pulls the drawing I made from his bag.

Grandpa immediately says, "That's a troll cross, all right. Those are used to keep a spirit at rest. I'm sure that's what they used on Coach Locke and his son. I wonder where the other talisman went?"

Marc and I both have the same, obvious question. "What does that mean to keep a spirit at rest?"

"So, in our heritage, it is believed that, when we die, we go to one of three places—Valhalla, Fólkvangr, or Hel—as you both should know by now," Grandpa explains. "It's also possible that the departed could return as ghosts, and that is what the talisman is used for—to keep the ghost away."

"No way. Are you saying that I could be seeing ghosts now?" I ask.

Grandpa shakes his head. "I'm not saying that at all, Jon. I'm just telling you what we believe *could* happen. If one or both of them came back as a ghost, they would be a *haugbui* or *draugr*. Either way, it could be trouble if their graves are disturbed. You didn't disturb them, did you?"

Marc and I look at each other, relieved, and then I say, "No, we left the graves alone out of respect for the dead."

"Good." Grandpa nods. "Leave them be."

"What do we do next?" I ask.

"*We* do nothing. I will get this vile to the APS to have it tested, and I'll tell them about the troll cross to see what they think that means. In the meantime, you two get back to going about your business as usual."

I have no idea how we're supposed to do that after what we just heard, but Marc and I do as we're told and head back to our next session as if nothing completely mind-blowing just happened.

As Marc and I walk, he turns to me and asks, "What do you know about *haugbui* or *draugr*?"

I shrug. "Nothing. I have never heard of them, either."

"I think we need to study up real quick on them."

I nod. "Agreed."

I think it's good news that Coach Locke is actually dead. I mean, a ghost can't be worse than the original person, can it? Maybe I have watched too many *Ghostbusters* or *Casper the Friendly Ghost* shows. Of course, there are plenty of other scary ghost examples out there, as well. Yeah, I need to study *haugbui* and *draugr* to find out what they are exactly capable of doing.

Campfire

Darla

THANKFULLY, THERE WERE no mishaps at the first-aid training today. We are getting close to having this merit badge knocked out! At least I will accomplish that if I do nothing else this week.

Afterward, Jenny and I head to the mess hall for dinner with Sam, Taylor, Marc, and Jon. We all catch each other up on our days. Sam and Taylor tell Marc and Jon about the frog incident, and they both think it's funny but seem really distracted. They keep whispering back and forth while the rest of us talk. I have no idea what they are talking about.

What could be more interesting than what is clearly becoming a prank war? Maybe they're plotting what they're going to do to us? Whether we intended to start a battle or not? It's clear that the game is on.

"You guys better be careful with the pranks," Marc warns. "We aren't allowed to do those anymore because they were getting out of hand."

We all completely ignore that. I'm sure everyone knows that pranks are still going to happen. Sometimes, you think they happened when, apparently, they did not. Although, I still know somebody was messing with us. Maybe it was Marc and Jon, and that's what they are whispering about. Nope, it wasn't Jon. He ran off into the woods. Unless maybe he circled back? I don't know, but somebody definitely messed with our tent.

After dinner, we head out to a lightly wooded area that is set up for playing Capture the Flag. This time, we aren't in pairs. Our two units will be squaring off against each other to determine the winner. Sam is the captain of the Blue Hill team, and Jon is the captain of our team. I would say the Grinwell team, but I'm not ready to give them that just yet.

Once we establish the territories and all the ground rules, I call a huddle for our team so we can discuss our strategy.

As I talk, it's clear that Jon isn't paying attention and isn't interested in leading this particular event. So, I happily step up. I ask everyone how fast they are and designate some of the fastest people to be seekers—aka. on offense—and the rest will be back defending our flag. We're going to seek in pairs so that, when someone comes after us, we can split up and at least one of us has a good chance of getting back to our side or possibly capturing the flag. This takes quite a while because, as it happens, these guys are all pretty good at this game. It's probably because of all the strategy they deploy in the various video games they play.

After about an hour, I start to wonder if we are going to have to just declare this a stalemate. About then, I have an idea for a coordinated attack. I send all but two of our seekers to one side of the field and tell them to run as fast as they can and don't stop. Meanwhile, Jon and I head down the other side and make our way toward their flag.

As Jon and I near the flag, their team catches on, and Sam is charging back our way. Jon grabs the flag and runs as fast as he can. Then he turns his back to Sam and fakes sticking the flag in his pocket while also pulling out his pocket liner as he really sneaks the flag to me. Then he yells, "Split up!"

He runs as fast as he can, as if he has the flag. Meanwhile, I have it tucked safely inside my front pocket as I head back to our side in a slightly different direction from Jon.

Sam heads straight for Jon and tags him well before he gets across the line to our side. Marc and Taylor are now chasing me and almost get me, but as they dive to touch me, I jump and cross the line to our side. *We made it!* We finally won, and Jon finally made a good strategic decision!

We all group together to celebrate our victory as Jon awkwardly offers me a high-five. I haven't had anyone give me a high-five in quite a long time.

"Oh, Jon, you certainly are an awkward mess sometimes, but great work on that fake. That was actually a really good idea."

"Gee, thanks for the compliment, I guess?"

I smile and offer a quick, "You're welcome." Then I head over to catch up with Jenny and rub the flag in Sam's face, literally. It sure feels good to finally get a win!

The last event of the evening is a campfire with s'mores, which sounds fantastic after running around for that long. I built back up somewhat of an appetite.

We all sit around the fire in clumps of five or six and just talk and eat. This is what camping and the Scouts is all about. I enjoy the accomplishments, whether it's winning an activity, learning new skills, or collecting badges. That's exactly why I joined.

Just like on the hike, I'm sitting next to Jon, and I decide to take the opportunity to bring up what I want to do next year.

"Jess is trying to get me to go out for the cheerleading team next year ... That's not what I have in mind or what I really want to do. I know it means a lot to her, though."

"Have you talked to her about it?" Jon asks. "Jess is pretty understanding, at least more so than most people."

I lower my head and shake out a no a couple of times.

"What is it you have in mind?"

"Promise not to laugh?" I ask.

"Promise."

"I really want to try out for the wrestling team," I confess. "I used to do jiu-jitsu, and I was decent at it. I think I could be a really good wrestler."

Jon doesn't hesitate to say, "You should go for it, Darla! If that's what you want, then you should talk to Jess and just go for it."

"It's not really that easy. My mother has made it clear that she is not interested in raising a tomboy and really wants me to focus on dance. Cheer is a natural choice in her mind, so I'm worried about my mother in addition to Jess."

"Then you have to talk to them both. You have to chase your passions and your dreams."

He's right.

I put my hand on his shoulder and tell him, "Thanks, Jon. You're a great listener."

We sit there a bit longer. Normally, it would be awkward to just sit with someone in silence but, for some reason, with Jon, it isn't. We look out at the water and enjoy the scenery.

Eventually, I turn to him and ask, "What are you staring at?"

"Oh, I'm just watching the lightning bugs go across the water."

I giggle. "The what? Do you mean the fireflies?"

Jon nods. "Yeah, well, all of us from around here call them lightning bugs."

"That's just silly. It's not like they fly around, shooting out lightning bolts from their butts."

"Well, they also don't fly around with fire coming out of their bottoms, right?"

Ha. Yeah, that's a good point.

I shake my head. "That's fair. Agree to disagree?"

He agrees.

I realize it's getting late, and I am beat, so I glance over at Jon and say, "I'm going to turn in for the night."

"Goodnight, Darla."

I smile. Then, from over my shoulder, I say, "Goodnight, Jon."

Ghost Stories

Jon

AS DARLA WALKS AWAY with Jenny, Marc sticks his elbow into my side and says, "Way to go, tiger!"

I shrug. "It's not really like that."

Marc rolls his eyes. "Sure, Jon, sure. I can see what is going on before my eyes just fine."

I can feel my face start to heat up again and decide to just say, "Whatever. I'm going back to the tent to do some reading."

"Knock yourself out. I'm going to have a few more s'mores."

I head over to Grandpa and ask, "You have anything that I can read about troll crosses and Asgardian spirits?"

We walk back to his tent, and he gives me what he has, along with some advice on where to start looking in our book of rhymes, as well.

There isn't too much on the subject, but I do come across enough to provide a fair amount of reading for the night. It's a good thing, too, because, right now, I don't feel like sleeping at all. I'm almost afraid to close my eyes until I know more about what could be happening. It's all just so overwhelming.

Let's start with what happens to an Asgardian when they die, at least here on Earth. Our beliefs say that they are going to end up in one of three realms. There is Valhalla, which is the realm of Odin, and this is where dead warriors drink, fight, and reminisce about their glory days. Then there is Fólkvangr, which is the "field of the people," but it's also a place where half of those who die in combat go. More importantly, it is the home of the fertility goddess, Freya. There is some debate here whether Fólkvangr is its own realm or a part of Valhalla, but for the matter at hand, it's not important. Finally, there is Hel, which is a dreary place where most of the souls go. And here's a shock; it's ruled by Loki's daughter with the same name, Hel. It sounds horrible, but this is where I imagine someone like Coach Locke would be destined to go. However, I'm sure that, if he had his way, he would be more likely to pick either of the other two realms. Most likely Fólkvangr, because of, well, Freya. That would make the most sense knowing the way his mind works. However, when I read further, it is possible that the souls stay here in this realm and haunt the living as ghosts.

The book talks about two specific types of ghosts. The first is a *haugbui*, which is a soul that stays around their grave or burial place to protect the goods that are inside of it. The only thing not clear right now is how far of an area that might cover. Is the entire area around Harmony Grove considered part of this burial mound, or is it just specific to the grave and its immediate surroundings? They are said to have an incredible appetite and may even eat a human that disturbs their grave. I wonder if that means they would eat ... say, a deer?

The other kind of soul is a *draugr*, which is a spirit that is large in stature, strong, always hungry, and can even shape-shift into any kind of animal. Okay, so if indeed what I am seeing is the spirit of Coach Locke, he could be either of these, from what I currently know. I'm going to need to study them both then figure out if he is one of these. It's also possible that the APS is wrong and he never died, that he somehow survived and isn't a ghost of any kind.

One of the recurring themes, as it relates to spirits in our Norse heritage, is that they are more likely to be upset, if they feel that they were disrespected in their death in any way. Let's say they didn't have a proper burial, or they weren't provided with everything that they felt should be in their grave. I have no doubt that Coach Locke is going to feel like he was cheated out of life and certainly cheated from a proper burial.

He wasn't burned. He wasn't celebrated. He was simply taken in pieces, along with his son, to a remote location and buried with a super basic grave marker, and that is that. It's really kind of sad, and if he wasn't such a terrible person, I would feel bad for him. He must have had some family somewhere, or some friends who might like to know he has passed so they can bury him properly, but that didn't happen. He was treated like waste that you simply dispose of and leave to rot. I'm sure he is mad at Marc, me, Grandpa, and definitely at the APS. This could be one seriously angry spirit that we have on our hands.

I decide to spend more time studying the troll cross that we saw so I can better understand its purpose and how it is supposed to work to keep spirits in check.

In general, troll crosses can be used to protect your home from spirits or worn to protect a person wherever they go. In the case of burial, though, they have a special meaning. They are meant to contain the spirit and block them from exiting their grave. It seems as though that should have been quite effective against even the angriest of ghosts. Yet, here we are, with me clearly seeing Coach Locke roaming around the camp.

I decide to study how Bragi have used troll crosses in the past and all the various rhymes that exist. There are rhymes that are tied to a troll cross medallion. Some of them are for using them against an evil being, including and up to sending them away in various ways to Hel. They all are dependent on the type of being that they are used against. This is something I'm going to need to be careful about, because a bad situation could get even worse if you use the wrong rhyme at the wrong time.

By the time I finish, I realize that it's now well past midnight and entering into the wee hours of the morning. I'm finally getting sleepy and decide to close my eyes for just a minute. What could possibly go wrong if I just take a little nap?

Middle of the Night

Darla

JENNY AND I HAVE A long, peaceful walk back to our tent, but as soon as we get inside, we have a lot to talk about. This has been a really great day, and I'm just so glad we joined the Scouts and came on this trip.

"What do you think is going to be the most memorable thing about being here?" I ask Jenny.

"For me, probably winning the canoe race with Sam."

I can see that.

"What about you?" she asks.

"Honestly, I'm not sure yet. It has been really fun and nice to get to know everyone in both troops."

"Anyone in particular?" Jenny asks.

Of course she already knows the answer to that.

"Yeah, maybe. We will see."

With that, I am physically and mentally exhausted. It has been a full but fun day, and I am ready to turn in for the night.

After getting cleaned up and ready for bed, we turn out the lights. That's to say, we literally turn off our flashlights and lie there in the pitch-black, listening to the sounds of crickets lulling us to sleep. It's not that different from any night on the farm for me, just not quite as comfortable as being in my bed. The sounds, though, they are familiar and welcome sleep.

Before long, I find myself wandering the halls of the school again. This time, I am with Jenny, Jess, Sam, Taylor, and Jon. *Jon?* This is new.

It's a relatively normal day at school, but I can't help but feel excited. Something big is coming up for me. Is it cheerleading tryouts or something else?

I say goodbye to everyone then rush to get ready for ...

Hey!

Suddenly, I feel a massive hand over my mouth as I wake up and, for a second, I am so disoriented that I do nothing. I'm pretty sure it's just Sam getting me back for the prank. *Whatever, Sam. I'm not going to react and give you what you want.*

I smell something pleasant with a sweet taste, and then I fall right back into sleep and right back to where I was going.

It's a wrestling tryout! I'm really doing it! I'm going to be a wrestler!

I feel the stares as I enter the wrestling room and, once again, I'm aware of how different I am. It's a feeling that I hate, but also that I am getting accustomed to. Yes, I am different than most other girls, and I am also completely fine with that, so leave me alone already. It motivates me to try even harder.

I start out wrestling the guys who are closest in size to me. I am holding my own with all of them. Then we switch, and I find myself facing off against a former state champion, but something is off with him. He smells really bad, and he is falling apart, literally. *Gross!*

I get him tied up, and then his arm falls off. Suddenly, someone is yelling at me, asking me what I'm doing. It's a deep, masculine voice that is getting louder and louder until I realize he is really yelling at me. Then I hear it more clearly as it booms in my head.

"Wake up, girl!"

Then I remember the hand over my mouth, and I try to move, but everything is just so heavy, and my eyes don't want to open.

I feel a large hand slap me across the face lightly at first, on each side, and then it starts getting harder until it really hurts.

I open my eyes and see a huge man staring back at me and scream as loudly as I can. This is pure panic at this point, with a surge of adrenaline

I start to flail as best I can. What is happening to me? Is this real or a nightmare?

I struggle, trying to move, but I'm all tied up, and it hurts. The more I move, the more it hurts until I finally stop. It's real.

I close my eyes for a second to try to collect myself.

Then I hear the voice clearly as I feel another slap across my face that leaves a distinct burning sensation, as if the right side of my face is on fire. It's real. As real as it gets!

I start crying, and then hear my dad's voice inside my head. "*You are Darla Towns, and you can handle anything that anyone throws at you.*"

I instantly stop and take a good look at the massive man staring at me. "What do you want with me? What are you planning to do to me?"

"Oh, I plan to use you to lure out Bragg. Plain and simple. I want Jon Bragg, and I want him to suffer."

"Why ...? Why Jon? Why didn't you just take Jon then?"

He laughs. "Because I want Jon to be afraid and, unfortunately, he is not going to be afraid if it's just him. He'll be much more afraid if he thinks he's going to lose someone special to him."

I scoff. "I'm not special to Jon. I'm just a member of his scout troop."

He gets visibly angry and yells, "Enough! I have seen the two of you. I have been watching you closely. He cares. He cares a lot!"

I stop protesting, as it seems to be getting me nowhere.

I don't know. Maybe Jon does care. I hope he does, but I also hope it's more than just him who will come to try to find me. I mean, he's nice, but it looks like I'm going to need more than just a boy's help to get out of this situation. I'm at least going to need someone like Sam, who is closer in size to this enormous man.

I decide to tell him, "You're lucky I'm tied up, because I know jiu-jitsu!"

He laughs again. "Oh, is that so?" He then unties me and says, "Give it your best shot."

I run for him and attempt a double leg takedown, and he just sprawls, and sprawls hard, driving me straight into the ground. Before I know it, he has me locked up tight in a rear naked choke.

I know there is no point, but I tap out of habit.

"This isn't a game, little girl. This is the *real* world!"

Before I know it, I fall into a deep sleep, and when I come to, I am tied back up, but even tighter this time. In addition, now my throat hurts from his show of force, and my body is protesting every movement.

I decide to ask him again, "Why Jon? What did Jon do to you?"

"You will find out soon enough, girly, soon enough indeed what Bragg did to me and my boy. *I will get retribution! Make no mistake! Now quiet! Just shut your trap!*"

I really want to keep talking and see what is going to happen, just out of spite, but the logical side of my brain kicks in, and I decide silence is my best option right now.

Think, Darla, think. You have to get out of this mess somehow. There has to be a way!

Maze

Jon

MARC AND I WAKE UP to a lot of noise outside of our tent. It's several of the leaders going around, checking each of the tents, looking for someone.

Skipper unzips our tent next and pokes his head in, asking, "Who's in the tent."

Both Marc and I announce ourselves.

"Is anyone else in here, boys?" Skipper asks.

We both say, "No sir."

Then I ask, "What's going on, sir?"

"One of our scouts is missing, and we are trying to find her."

My mind starts racing because he said *her*, which can only mean Darla or Jenny. However, knowing who I think is out there, I know immediately it must be Darla.

Before he leaves, I ask, "Is it Darla?"

As he is about to zip the door, he says, "Yes, Jon. Let us know if you see or hear from her, okay, boys?"

"Of course, sir. Should we organize a search party?"

"Head to the mess hall, and we will get this all sorted out and come up with a plan."

We nod then get ready as quickly as we can so we can meet the others.

"Do you think it's Coach Locke?" Marc says.

"Yes, I'm afraid so. We need to find Grandpa."

Once we get up to the mess hall, we look around for Grandpa and run into Sam and Taylor, who are both comforting Jenny, who is distraught. She didn't hear anything last night; she just woke up and Darla was gone.

As of right now, we don't know if she went for a hike and got lost or if she has fallen somewhere and is hurt. We just have no idea. Of course, there are all kinds of theories being thrown around by the guys. None of which are logical or likely. Then again, maybe they aren't that crazy. After all, I think she may have been taken by a decedent of Loki or his ghost, so I really shouldn't be talking. Then again, I know what I saw, and I know it has to be him now.

As soon as everyone is there, we split up, using the buddy system, with the less experienced hikers teaming up with leaders so we can all fan out and look for Darla. Marc and I have a lot of experience, so we are allowed to head out on our own.

Before we leave, we stop to talk to Grandpa, who says, "Be careful, boys. Keep your eyes peeled and don't make any hasty decisions. I'm going to contact the APS and ask them for their assistance. Promise me you two will stick together."

"We promise, Grandpa."

Seeing as I saw Locke by the mess hall, Marc and I decide to head in the direction that I saw him running.

After walking around several of the places that I had already been, I decide to get a little smarter and say a rhyme to power my compass.

"Help this compass to point the way toward where Darla went last night.
Follow the trail that Locke has taken until her location is within my sight."

With that, the compass sets the direction, and Marc and I follow it. We walk for what seems like forever before we realize we are making a gigantic circle, or possibly circles. This is not something I am prepared for. My magic has never let me down.

"I don't understand," I tell Marc. "I wonder why we keep going in circles."

"Maybe Locke took her all around the area in an attempt to throw you off if you tried to use your magic?"

I slap my hand against my forehead. "Of course! I didn't think of that. Man, Locke is just too good at this. It seems like he has somehow gotten even better." I describe more of what I read last night to Marc so he could try to help me decide what type of spirit Locke has become, if we can confirm his death.

"I feel like we don't know enough," Marc says. "Let's keep following the trail and keep an eye out for anything suspicious."

We walk for another half hour or so before I stop and drop to my knees. "This is all my fault."

"What is all your fault?" Marc asks.

"He wouldn't have taken Darla if he didn't see her with me. It's *my fault* that she's in danger right now." I am beside myself as I realize what I'm saying is true.

Marc disputes this. "No, no, it's *not* your fault. This is all on Locke. You didn't do anything wrong, Jon. Just like you didn't do anything wrong when he decided to take me."

I appreciate it, but reply, "I may not have done anything wrong, but I know he took her because he wants me to come and try to find her."

"Well, maybe we shouldn't give him what he wants then."

"I know, but I just have to. There is no way I'm going to leave her out here, whether it's what he wants or not. Whether it's a trap or not. I have to find her. I have to make this right!"

Marc nods once. We are in agreement again.

We continue searching on, and we will do so until this nightmare is over.

Even with the compass that is being driven by magic, the woods have suddenly become a big, confusing maze. We keep running into dead ends near the water and have to circle back to find another path that we can take. It's doubtful that Locke stayed on a path, though, so we eventually abandon the paths altogether and start moving in large circles inward until we cover as much ground as possible while still following the compass.

We have been in these woods so many times that it's hard to imagine getting lost, but the more we do, the more confusing it seems to get. It's a good thing we have our compasses. We are going to need them to find our way back to camp. As of right now, without the compass, I would have no idea what direction I needed to go.

I am certain that Locke is getting a good laugh at this. I'm looking forward to putting an end to this forever. I just want to put Locke behind me.

Why won't he let go and leave this realm? He might run into the original Loki in another realm. *Ugh*. One of them is bad enough; can you imagine what a bunch of them would be like? Hel must have tons of fury with the likes of every Loki being her responsibility to contain.

Feeling Vulnerable

Darla

AS I SIT HERE, I CAN'T help but start to cry again. I have never felt so alone in my life. I cannot believe this is really happening to me. What did I do to cause someone to pick me out of all the people at the camp? Why me? Jon is friends with a lot of people. In fact, why not Marc? Marc is Jon's best friend. If he's going to care about anyone, it's going to be Marc.

Just as my entire body starts shaking from sobbing, I fall back on the words my dad said. I have to be strong. I have to keep my wits about me to get out of this alive. I need to take in my surroundings and try to figure out where I am.

It's dark, damp, and below my feet is just dirt. There is no floor here, there are no walls that I can see or feel. All I feel everywhere is dirt. I am below ground, that much is for sure.

I keep having rounds of panic attacks then realize this is not helping. Now I am starting to be afraid of what will happen if the ceiling or walls collapse on me. Plus, how is anyone going to find me below ground? How am I supposed to figure out where I am? How am I supposed to signal to anyone that I need help? Nope, I'm going to have to try to reason with this man and find out more about him. So, I decide to ask him some questions. It's a risk to even get his attention, but I have to try something.

"Sir? Excuse me, sir."

"What is it now, *girl*?"

No matter how many times I hear him say that, in such a degrading way ...

I have to stop letting it get to me. He's just so incredibly rude.

"Darla. My name is Darla."

"I don't care, *girl*."

There it is again. He's just a complete jerk.

I decide to try some flattery of sorts.

"Can I ask where you learned jiu-jitsu? You seem really good at it."

He laughs. "Girl, I've been a wrestler for most of my life. I even won an Olympic gold medal. In fact, I was one of the best wrestlers that ever walked this realm."

Realm? Who talks like that?

Suddenly, I remember the clipboard and the stories about the wrestling coaches from Grinwell.

"I remember hearing about you and how you just suddenly disappeared. Where have you been? Where has your son been?"

That was a mistake, because he gets really mad.

"I have been trapped underground, and it's all because of Bragg!"

Okay, I need to stop asking him questions, but how is it possible that Jon trapped this huge man anywhere, let alone underground. And, why would he even do that? This makes no sense at all. Then again, crazy isn't supposed to make sense. It's kind of the point of crazy. I think, when it comes to that, this guy is as sharp as they come.

I fall silent and let it go ... for now.

What was the story again about the wrestling team last year? One of the coaches was killed by a wild animal in the woods while he was hunting. Was it here at Harmony Grove? Can you even hunt here? Then the other coach, who is clearly this guy, came from somewhere near Des Moines, was an Olympic wrestler, and his son was a state champion. I remember him for sure from when we lived in West Des Moines. He was a huge underdog at the start of the year and, by the end of the year, he was virtually unstoppable. It was really motivating. At least the story I saw on the news was inspiring.

I wonder where his son is right now. He's clearly not here, and I'm not sure I want to bring that up. Something tells me it's not going to make him any calmer, and I really don't want him to get any more agitated than he already is. It's completely unnerving.

Still, something else seems off with this guy. I mean, in addition to being a kidnapper. He's scary in every way and seems to be completely fixated on whatever he's doing. How can he even see well enough down here to be doing anything at all? Also, how did he find this place?

He seems to be digging with his hands, but he must not be getting anywhere, because he just keeps throwing his hands up in frustration. Maybe he ran into some rock, or some tree roots, or who knows? It could be anything.

I'm starting to get hungry and thirsty, so I decide to ask him, "Do you have any food or water?"

He grunts. "No, *girl.* I don't have anything down here for you. I go up there when I need to eat something, but you aren't going to be needing anything for long."

That terrifies me. There can be only one reason why I'm not going to need anything. He is going to kill me. This is it. I'm never going to see anyone again. Not my parents, not Jenny, not Jess, and not Jon. I am going to die here, all alone.

This takes a moment to fully settle in, but if that's true, then I really don't have anything to lose.

"Then get on with it already! If you're going to kill me, then *do it*! Just get it over with already!"

He roars with laughter. I guess this is exactly what he wanted.

"What would be the fun in that? I want Bragg to see me kill you. He *has* to be here and bring me what I need, or this will all be for nothing!"

Unable to let this go, I ask, "Why me? Why not Marc or his grandpa? You know they were both at the camp, too, right?"

He shrugs. "I have already dealt with both of them, and Grandpa Bragi and Baby Thor are of no interest to me. I already did what I needed to do to them."

What does that mean? Apparently, there is a lot more to this story than I know.

"What ...? What are you talking about?" I stammer, thinking he killed them already.

"Ask your boyfriend when he gets here."

"He's not my boyfriend!" I shout.

He smirks. "Sure, girl, whatever you say. Again, I don't really care. He cares about you, and that's enough. You'll find out everything soon enough."

"What makes you so sure he'll find me?"

"Oh, he'll find you. You just wait, girl, you just wait ... He can't help trying to be the hero."

Ha, Jon the hero? That's not what immediately comes to my mind when I think of Jon.

The Lake

Jon

WHATEVER WE DO AND whatever path we take, we continue to end up back at the water. We have been at this for quite a while now, and I'm getting nervous about what is happening to Darla. She must be so scared. I also have no idea what Locke is going to do with her. It would help a lot if I even knew what he was. Is he a ghost? If he is, which I guess is possible, then what kind?

After studying all the possibilities last night, it's critical that I know. If I use the wrong rhyme on him, then he could get even stronger. He might even get strong enough to pull some or all of us into another realm *with* him. I have to find him, and I have to find him now!

I turn to Marc. "We're getting nowhere."

He nods. "I'm aware. What were you saying about the different types of ghosts?"

I restate everything I know about the *haugbui* and *draugr*, and how they tend to protect their burial mounds.

"You think he's over on the other side of the lake by the graves we saw?"

"Of course!" I reply. "That makes so much sense. How did we not think of that sooner? Let's go find out!"

I try to decide if we should tell Grandpa where we are going, but I have no idea where he is right now. I know we said we wouldn't do anything hasty, but I'm not sure this qualifies. After all, we've already been over there before, and we didn't really see anything. This is probably nothing. I mean, we saw two graves, and they both looked undisturbed, so there is no harm in just going over to double-check.

Marc and I get into the canoe and quickly head toward the other side of the lake.

Everything we do right now seems to be taking hours instead of minutes. I'm just so worried, because Locke could be heading anywhere, and the more time that passes, the farther away he could be. Of course, if he is a *haugbui* or *draugr*, then he is bound to some limit. So, I hope he is one of those things—at least he can't get too far away from Harmony Grove.

This whole thing is so much more complicated than I could ever have imagined. I don't understand how it's possible. I killed him, and I killed Dustin. That should be the end of the story. How is he on the loose, and why is he not bound to his grave by a troll cross if he was dead when the APS placed him there?

When we get back to where we saw the graves, we see the troll cross still on the one grave marker so that has not been disturbed. That's when realization hits. The other grave also must have had a troll cross, and somehow that one is gone. That is the one we need to find.

We search around the graves, but we can't find anything. We start making wider and wider circles around the grave as we fan out, trying to find something, anything that could lead us to where Locke has taken Darla, or to where the other troll cross is. We keep finding nothing, but the compass is still circling us around the graves. Except now it keeps taking us back to a specific tree that is closest to the grave without the talisman.

"Search the ground really carefully around this tree," I tell Marc. "There must be something here because this thing keeps directing us back here."

There is a lot of debris around this tree. Lots of branches, lots of thick grass, and it's kind of gross, to be honest. We both have our hands spread out, though, trying to find *anything* on the ground around it.

"Jon, I think I found something!"

I head over to him, seeing a big piece of wood that is buried a bit in the debris, but it seems to be a makeshift door of some sort.

I look at Marc. "Nice job! Why don't you head back across the lake and let Grandpa know what we found?"

"No way!" Marc exclaims. "We promised to stick together, remember?"

I shake my head. "Marc, there's no time to argue. I need to stay here and figure out how to get down there, and you need to go get help."

"I don't know, Jon. This seems wrong."

"Just do it, Marc. Please?"

He relents, heading back to the canoe while telling me, "Okay, but don't do anything stupid while I'm gone. And if Grandpa gets mad, it's on you. I'll get back as fast as I can."

Of course I have every intention of getting this taken care of right now. If Locke is down there, and if he has Darla down there, I can't waste any more time. I have to see, and then I have to get her out!

In order to deal with Locke, however, I have to find his troll cross, which I now suspect he has in his possession. How he got it is still a mystery to me, but to leave his grave, he must be in command of his troll cross. My guess is someone found the graves and, for some reason, attempted to take the talisman, thinking it was cool. I must admit that the thought did cross our mind, too, when we saw that one, but that is obviously disrespectful. That would have instantly freed Locke, and he no doubt killed the person in possession of his troll cross so he could take it for himself. Even with that, it would only give him the ability to move around his burial mound.

I wonder if I can use the other troll cross, or if that would free Dustin. I assume that's where he's buried, but I have no idea if he stuck around in this realm or not. I guess that's a risk that I'm simply going to have to take. I need something, and I'm not going down this hole without some form of protection.

I grab the troll cross, move the piece of wood aside, and then I start to walk down a slanted slope into pitch black darkness.

The Cat

Darla

IT HAS BEEN EERILY quiet for a while now. My eyes have somewhat adjusted to the darkness, so I can see a little bit in front of me. I can see enough to know that he is clawing at a wall, but nothing is happening to it. It's like he hit concrete, but it looks just like every other wall down here. Whatever it is, it is making him irate. He wants through that barrier.

I hear him whisper, "Hold on. I'm coming soon."

Coming for who? This guy has totally lost it. Now he is talking to dirt walls!

Just then, I hear a noise come from somewhere else, but before I can let out a scream, he is in front of me in an instant, his hand over my mouth, pressing so hard that it really hurts. It feels like someone punched me in the face and covered my mouth at the same time.

My eyes immediately start watering, and all I can do is gasp in shock. That. Hurt.

"Shh ... Someone's here. With any luck, it's your boyfriend." Then he punches me so hard that I hit my head on the side of the dirt wall next to me and fall back into the darkness.

As I go down, I am completely aware of the fact that, with every fraction of a second, I am losing my chance to be saved by a scream. It just cannot come out.

Right before I'm completely out, I see something crazy. I see him turn into a black cat and head off in the direction of the noise I heard. That's silly. Why a cat?

OPENING MY EYES, I recognize a stabbing pain on the side of my head and remember what happened. I'm gagged but with something else around my mouth. A cloth, I think. Since my hands are tied, all I can do is grunt and try to make any noise I can to draw the attention of whatever I heard earlier.

Then I feel something beside me, and it's purring. Ah, the cat. That makes more sense. I wish I could pet this little guy. I can't tell you how much I appreciate anything other than that man around me.

It's almost like this little kitty is scared or something. It's hiding behind my leg and purring quite loudly. Cats are so weird.

One thing that has always freaked me out about cats is their eyes change considerably in the dark, and this one has especially wild eyes, almost like they are glowing. At least it's some much-needed comfort after what has been an incredibly traumatic experience.

I'm hungry, thirsty and, up until now, I was feeling completely alone. I'll take one of those being satisfied over none any time. My new little buddy.

I decide it's time to attempt another escape. I start to squirm however I can. I can move my feet, but my legs are tied. I can move my fingers, but my hands are tied behind my back. I can breathe, but my mouth is gagged. No matter what I do, I cannot seem to move away from this spot, so I guess that means I'm also tied to something. Great. I'm stuck.

There must be something I can do. *Think, Darla, think.*

Can I swing my legs up? Let's try that.

I swing my legs up and over my head, and they run smack into what feels like tree roots. A lot of twisted-up tree roots, which must be what I am tied to. Okay, well, at least I know that. I try to swing my legs back down without landing on my new furry friend. This little guy seems to not to mind it down here at all.

As soon as I get back down, he jumps up into my lap and just stares at me. I guess that'll keep my legs in place for a while.

Okay, cat. Now what?

I move just enough to get him off my lap, and he meows in disapproval. Hmm ... Well, if I cannot make noise, maybe this cat can make some.

I try to bump him as best I can to see if he will do it again, but he just moves out of the way before I can even get to him. So, now even the cat is outsmarting me.

I try to see if I can scoot enough to sit on his tail, and just as I get over there, he hisses and claws my arm. Ouch, that really hurt. And now even the cat is not happy with me.

He decides he wants nothing to do with me and heads off into the darkness. That leaves me back alone again, sitting in the dark and just waiting for the inevitable return of that man to do whatever he wants to me. This is what hopeless feels like.

You think you know what it's like, but sadly, you really don't until it's too late. At this point, there is nothing left for me to do but wait and hope that this ends soon, one way or the other. I know I'm not supposed to give up hope, but I can't help it. I feel as helpless as a little girl right now. No, I feel like a baby who can do absolutely nothing to help herself. I am exactly what I never wanted to become. This is the worst. The absolute rock bottom.

Just then, the little cat comes running back over to me, and I have never been so excited to see anything before in my life! I thought he was gone forever.

I'm so sorry, cat. I promise I won't do anything else. Just don't leave me here alone again, please. If I could talk to you, I would apologize. But, as you can see, I'm gagged.

Ha, I'm now not just talking at a cat, I am pretending that I am having a full-on conversation with him. I must be getting delirious. It's a cat. Right now, though, it is a gloriously wonderful cat that has at least chosen not to leave me alone for now.

Can he hear what I am thinking? It's worth a shot.

Meow. Meow. Meow.

Be as loud as you can be. Please be as loud as you can be.

Right at that point, he starts doing it, making a lot of noise, and my heart skips a beat. Surely someone can hear that. Whomever that man went after must be able to hear this cat now.

Come on; save me. I'm here, and I need you. Just like I need this cat.

Good job, cat. Keep it up. Please!

Meanwhile, he is looking in the direction that the man ran, as if he cannot wait for someone to arrive, too. I love this cat right now like I have never loved anything before! My feline hero!

Fireflies

Jon

THE HOLE IS DEEP AND wide. Wide enough for Locke to get down carrying Darla. It seems like I'm going down several feet. How much farther can we even go without breaking through to water or something else?

By the time I get to the bottom, I can see a small circle of light back in the direction that I walked, and it looks like I can go two different ways right now.

To my right, I get the distinct smell of death. To my left, all I see is pitch black. I'm not sure what to do. I didn't expect to go underground, so I didn't bring a flashlight. I mean, it's daytime; why would I need one?

All I can think about right now is finding Darla. She's down here because of me. We were just together last night, talking at the campfire about ... fireflies.

Wait a minute! Yes, fireflies!

"If you can hear me from above this hole that has been dug,
Please send me down some friendly lightning bug.
I would take two or three.
Actually, as many as you can spare,
So I can see."

It takes about a minute, but I see first one, and then a whole family of lightning bugs that have come to my rescue.

Look at that! That is kind of beautiful.

Even though I really don't want to know what that smell is to the right, and I am seriously dreading it, I need to rule that direction out first. So, my new friends and I head that way.

What we find are the remains of a lot of different animals that have been killed various ways and are all mostly eaten. I suppose Locke has been hungry over the last several months and didn't want to leave a trail of dead animals above ground. One would think he would bury them or dispose of them some other way, but I guess he doesn't take as much offense to dead smelling things as I do. In any event, there is nothing left to see this way, so we can head back the other direction, just me and my fireflies.

It quickly becomes apparent that this is quite an extensive system of tunnels that has taken Locke a while to construct. Then I reach several forks in the path and realize that some of the paths lead to dead ends. Either he hasn't constructed the entire system, or this is intentionally a maze. Either way, it's not good. It's not good at all.

I drop to my knees again to see if I can hear anything at all coming from any direction if I close my eyes. That's when I hear what sounds like a muffled cat. It must be a ways away, but that is definitely a cat meowing.

That's certainly strange. What would a cat be doing down here? Maybe it came in here to catch a rat or some other rodent? It's hard to say, but it's my only possible lead right now.

Let's see if we can find this cat.

The irony is not lost on me. This is like a cat and mouse game, and I feel like the mouse running through the maze, trying to find the cat. Everything about this seems wrong, but it's clear that this is Locke's doing.

The cat stopped making noises for quite a while, so I am not able to find it through my hearing. I resume trying each path until I reach a dead end then circle back until I try each route. This is going to take a while, but I have to be thorough. Darla could be down any one of these, and I'm not going to make the mistake of missing the right one.

One thing strange that I notice is, every time I hit a dead end, the troll cross is drawn to the wall. It's like it wants to literally go through the wall and get to the other side. It feels like a strong magnetic pull, but that's obviously not the case. Whatever I am walking around and constantly running into is important to this thing. That makes whatever is behind these walls significantly more appealing to me. My curiosity is beyond piqued, but I need to stay focused on finding the right path, because Darla obviously didn't walk through a dirt wall to get anywhere.

After a few more minutes of no sound and no help, I hear the cat again. It is loud this time and not stopping. *Perfect! Keep it up cat! I'm coming.*

This helps significantly, even though I have to pass multiple paths on my way toward the meows.

As I get closer, my heart starts to pound a little faster. I am at least making some progress now.

After a few more turns, I see something up ahead. I send some of the fireflies forward so I can have a better look. Is that the cat? Is someone tied up next to the cat? I start to run, but then I see this is an opening, so I slow down and drop to my knees. I don't want to run straight into a trap. If Locke is in there, he could hit me before I know it.

Just then, whoever is tied up sees me and starts to make noises. Lots of noises. I have no choice but to get closer.

It's her!

I'm so happy that I drop everything and fall to my knees to give her a hug. "I thought I was never going to see you again!"

Just then, the cat quickly comes over to me and grabs the troll cross that I had just set down in its mouth. Then it changes before my eyes back into Locke.

"I'll take that. Thank you very much, Bragg!"

Before I know it, he jumps on me and slaps his enormous hand over my mouth. I try to bite down, but all I get is air.

He laughs. "Not this time, Bragg!" He slides a gag around my mouth then proceeds to beat me.

I don't know how it's possible, but he is even stronger than he used to be. Every punch feels like I'm being hit by a ton of bricks. I struggle to breathe, and I know this could be it.

I hear Darla crying. She is so distraught and panicking. I realize she is going to witness my death that feels like it's coming sooner rather than later. But, just then, Locke stops.

"Soon enough, Bragg. First, I must tend to my boy. He needs to see this. Don't worry; I'll be right back. You two stay right where you are." He cackles as he walks out, back into the darkness, leaving me bleeding and dragging myself over to where Darla is to check on her. I can barely move, though, and need a minute to start to heal.

As my eyes start to close, Darla tries her best to get my attention and to keep me awake. I slip into darkness, however, despite my best efforts, not knowing what I will wake up to or if I will wake up this time.

I'm sorry, Darla. I'm sorry, Marc. I'm sorry, Grandpa.

Out of My Mind

Darla

WHEN I SEE JON COMING down that tunnel, lit by what I think are dozens of fireflies, my heart skips a beat. This is quite the entrance, even if I am somehow dreaming. This is perfect! Forget a knight in shining armor! Try a Boy Scout being led by fireflies!

The man is not here, but Jon is, so I start making as much noise as I can. I grunt, I scream, I do everything I can to let him know I am right here.

When he drops to his knees to hug me it is the best feeling in the world. I then question whether this is a mirage or not, because the cat sitting next to me , the cat that befriended me and helped lead Jon to me, grabs something off the ground in his mouth right before turning into the man before my eyes. Now I know for a fact, I am *completely* out of my mind. I just saw a tiny black cat turn into a gigantic man. How is that possible?

Great. Now I am getting delirious and seeing things. That is not exactly what I needed right now. I thought Jon must be an illusion, too, but then I see the blood as he is beaten, and that is all too real. I gasp as he is brutally attacked, and I feel my heart sinking with every blow Jon takes. Now he is in just as bad of a situation as I am. Possibly worse. That man desperately wants to kill Jon.

When he stops and leaves, he tells us he will be back to get his boy. I had no idea anybody else was down here. He must be a chip off the old block, though, if he is down here and did nothing this whole time.

Jon barely makes his way over to me, and I can tell he is in extreme pain. I try everything I can think of to keep him awake, but he finally gives in and collapses right next to me with his face hitting the ground hard.

I try to get closer to him, but we are still too far away from each other. I can't even touch him right now. *Jon, why did you come down here by yourself? You should have brought the others with you! What were you thinking?*

Before too long, the man is back and has tools with him—a shovel, a pick, and other things that he must have used to dig these tunnels. He starts attacking the wall, tearing through it like it's nothing. With every swing of the pick, he takes out a large chunk of earth as he makes yet another tunnel. Where is he going this time? I thought he was going after his boy?

The noise suddenly stops as he drops his pick, and then I hear him say, "Locke, where are you?"

Then I hear a younger voice respond, "Coach? Is that you?"

"Sure thing, son." He then leads him back into the area where Jon and I are being kept.

The boy asks, "What is *he* doing here?"

"Well, he brought your talisman, son, so I could free you."

"Why would he do something stupid like that?" the boy asks.

The man points at me. "For her."

"Who is *she*? I have never seen her around here before."

"Go ask her yourself."

The boy comes over to me. "Who are you?"

The man laughs at him. "You have to take her gag out, Locke."

The boy reaches up to remove the fabric from my mouth, but his hand passes right through it.

The man laughs. "Ha, you can't do it like that. You have to do it this way." Then he smacks my face, and I feel the burning again as the fabric falls from my mouth.

I scream, “Ouch! That hurt!”

“Answer the boy. Tell him who you are!”

“I am Darla Towns, and I live in Blue Hill.”

“Well, Darla Towns,” the boy says, “you sure have bad taste in guys if you like this one.” He points to Jon then kicks him, but again, his foot goes right through Jon.

This makes the man laugh again. “You need to eat. After you eat, you will be corporeal.”

“Let’s start with her!” The boy points to me, but the man shakes his head.

“Trust me; you don’t want to taste that one. She isn’t right. She’s salty like the sea, and we aren’t going there yet. Let’s go hunting real quick then come back to finish Bragg off together.”

“Let me just eat Bragg then.”

“You cannot handle an Asgardian. You will not even break his skin. Just listen to me. Let’s go!”

The boy submits. “Yes, sir. As long as it isn’t one of your green, superfood shakes, Coach.”

Coach laughs and shakes his head. Then they head down the tunnel that Jon came from, together, like a normal father and son walking off to go have a completely normal meal together.

As soon as they are gone, I try to wake up Jon. Fortunately, they didn’t gag me again, so I can talk now.

“Jon, wake up.” I keep saying that until I get pretty loud and am screaming at him. “Jon, wake up! Wake up now!”

He starts to stir a little, still badly hurt.

“Come closer to me, Jon.”

He shakes his head ever so slightly, and I recognize that he is giving up.

“Oh no, you’re not, Bragg. You are *not* giving up on me, on us, not now!”

With that, he moves a little at a time, just kind of inch-worms his way over to me.

"Just a little closer, Jon."

He reaches me, and then his head falls again, but into my lap this time. Now that he is close enough for me to reach, I bend forward as much as I can and am once again thankful for my flexibility. I use my teeth to loosen the gag that is tied around his mouth. It takes a while because it's tied tight. The man made sure this thing didn't fall off him. I can't get it all the way off, but I manage to loosen it. It must have also been enough to wake Jon, because I hear him start up with his poetry again.

"Not now, Jon. Now is not the time for poetry. Just breathe and try your best to stay awake."

I hear him say,

"Please give me the strength that I need to heal my wounds and to restore me,
So I can prepare for battle with the next Loki I see."

As I watch, I see his wounds start to heal. His cuts, bumps, and quite possibly broken bones all seem to return to normal. Before I know it, he is standing up, looking down at me.

"Thank you. That's all the help I needed." He reaches down and unties me from the tree roots, and then I am in his arms.

I have no idea what is going on. I am either hallucinating or Jon literally just performed some amazing magic before my eyes. I pinch myself just to make sure this is real, and then I say, "Ouch. Yep, this is real."

"I would love to stay and explain this to you, but I think now is a really great time for us to get the heck out of here. What do you say?"

I start to run first and say from over my shoulder, "I thought you'd never ask," and keep running until I get about a foot into the darkness and run into a stone wall. Nope, it's him. He's back.

I just scream. There isn't much else to do at this point.

He grabs me and tells Jon, "Back off, Bragi, or I'll snap this little girl's neck."

Jon takes a step back, and then something, or someone, comes rushing in and crashes into Jon, taking him down. It's the boy from earlier, and now they're fighting each other.

I see the boy figured out whatever his physical problem was. Now he is wrestling and punching Jon with renewed passion and full force. Yet again, Jon is losing another battle.

Come on, Jon. Do something! Anything! I believe in you ... For some reason, I believe in you.

The Whole Truth

Jon

AS DUSTIN AND I FIGHT each other, and each get some substantial blows in, we hear Locke yell, "Enough!"

That gets Dustin's attention and gets him off me.

"Hold the girl," Locke tells Dustin. "If Bragi tries any rhymes, snap her neck, and I mean immediately. Got it?"

"Yes, Coach, got it!" Dustin seems all too ready to do it, too.

"Leave Darla out of this. You know no good can come from having her see this, right?"

"See what?" Darla asks.

That's when Locke decides to tell the whole story, or at least his side of it.

"Girl, this boy here is a descendant of Bragi. Do you know who Bragi was in the old world?"

Darla shakes her head. "No, never heard of him. I do know his last name is Bragg, though. Is that somehow the same thing?"

Locke shakes his head. "The school system is such a shame. They don't even bother teaching proper history. Bragi was a son of Odin. The second eldest after Thor. He was the god of poetry and manipulated people and things with his words. Bragg has that same power, and he used that sharp tongue of his to kill me and my son. For that, he will pay dearly. As will you! In fact, I intend to start with you!"

I protest, "That's not the whole truth!"

"By all means, then why don't you tell her? She deserves to know why she's going to die, but leave out any of your poetry, boy. Don't push me!" Locke snarks.

I turn to Darla. "This man standing before you is a descendant of the infamous Loki. You know who Loki is, right?"

"Of course I know who Loki is!"

"Well, at least they are teaching about the most important gods and giants from the old world!" Locke says with a smug glance over at me.

I continue, "So, the Loki line of thieving and cunning *giants* has always had trouble obeying Asgardian laws. They abused their powers for centuries and were warned time and time again. Eventually, they were stripped of their powers, which is a matter Asgardians take very seriously. We thought that was the end of their line, but one of them figured out how to extract the blue essence from other Asgardians to temporarily give them their powers back. Then they, and specifically this man, decided to start hunting us down to extract our essence so he could continue to abuse his powers.

"He came to Grinwell after almost killing my grandpa to take his essence. He came to find *me*. Instead, he found Marc and thought that, because everyone called him Baby Thor that *he* was the Asgardian. They captured him, much like they did you, and tortured him until I came to break him out. At that time, in order to save my life and Marc's, I used a blood rhyme to kill these two. So, he is telling the truth there. I did kill these giant tricksters, but he left me no choice!" I trail off as if I am asking for forgiveness as I glance over at Darla, "I had no choice."

"Enough! enough of the giant talk!" Locke starts to pace back and forth. "Your APS as usual, has it all wrong, Bragi! Do you realize that giants and gods, at one point in time, not only co-existed but many married and many had children together? You might be surprised that you, and even your precious Thor, have a significant amount of giant essence flowing through you. In fact, Thor was more than three quarters giant!"

I look at him. "Yeah, yeah, yeah. I know all about this, Locke. I have studied everything I could about our history, and I also know that, if you hadn't tricked Balder's brother into shooting him with a mistletoe arrow, the gods and giants never would have fought, and Ragnarök would not have happened. At least not when it did, if ever! All of the hatred, all of the fighting, and all of the ill-will between gods and giants is solely *your* fault. Well, Loki's fault and, by relation, your fault!"

"Oh, come on, Bragi; you give us Loki far too much credit," Locke replies. "Yes, Loki pulled some little tricks on Odin and Frigg, but they chose to pursue it, and they could have left it alone."

"Loki, conned Frigg into revealing the one thing that could harm Balder, and Loki not only crafted an arrow out of that one material—mistletoe—but he cowardly chose to convince Balder's blind brother into sending it into his heart. That's *a lot* more than a little trick!"

Locke shrugs. "Still, the gods had a chance to take your precious high road, and they sought revenge instead. So, tell me. How are they any better than the giants they used to love?"

I admit, "Mistakes were made, but since Ragnarök, we have done our best to live peacefully and to help humans as much as possible."

Locke interrupts, "Because you had to! Don't think you or the other Asgardians are any better than the giants. After all *you* have killed, as well!"

Darla, doing the best she can to follow all of this, extends her hands toward him and says, "But, Jon, he's right here. You didn't actually kill him."

Locke laughs. "That's where you're wrong, *girl*!" He starts shape-shifting into different creatures then finally comes back to his human form. "I am a ghost, as is the boy holding you right now."

Darla laughs. "Are you guys all putting me on right now? What is this?"

Locke gets right up in her face. "It. Is. Not. Funny, girl!" When he says it, his head gets about four times larger than it was and her eyes do the same.

She looks over at me, and I shrug and point at him. "I'm afraid it's true, Darla. He is no longer a chaos-loving giant. He is now a *haugbui*."

Locke turns back to me. "Nice guess, Bragi. But I am no *haugbui*!"

"Well, either way, he's a spirit. It's true." I'm trying to not let on that I know he is a *draugr* now. Deep inside, though, I am excited and scared at the same time, knowing what this means. At least I can start thinking about how I can take them down. If he is a draugr, I'm going to need both his and Dustin's troll crosses to pull this off and take them both down.

Still processing she says, "I'm not saying I believe all this. I'm more likely to believe this is a huge nightmare and *none* of this is real, but ... let's say it *is* real. What is the end game here?"

Locke rushes me. "We intend to end this Bragi and send him to Hel where he belongs."

"I'm sorry I asked," Darla mumbles.

By then, Locke is on top of me, holding my mouth shut with one hand and laying into me with the other. He certainly knows how to fight. This has never been his problem. It's always the same with this one.

When he grabs me from behind to pull me over his head, I feel something on his chest and around his neck. *Aha*! That must be where his troll cross is hanging.

I know I can't say a rhyme without risking Darla's life, so I have to do my best to survive this scuffle right now.

As I escape his grip, Locke says, "You've been training, Bragi. Good! This will be much more interesting this time."

As we struggle for positions on each other, I reach up and grab at his chest, pulling hard. This causes the troll cross to fall to the ground and that infuriates Locke.

"Not so easy, Bragi!" He throws me across the room.

I start to say a rhyme, and then I remember that I can't. I look over at Dustin to make sure he hasn't done anything.

Locke looks over at him, too. "What did I say? What are you waiting for? Did you not hear him start with his words? Why is *she* still alive?"

Dustin throws her to the ground. "Because I have no problem with her. I see what you saw in her now. I know, Coach."

This gives me just enough time to make a run for Dustin. Before I get there, though, Darla has already taken him down.

I rip at his chest and throw his troll cross on the ground next to his father's. Just as Locke is going to reach for them, I hear Grandpa and the APS arrive. Finally, what took them so long!

Locke diverts his attention and dives at Darla, who steps to the side to narrowly escape. Dustin and Locke get to their feet, and they start to literally grow in size, to where they barely fit in the tunnel. Yep, they are most definitely *draugr*. They scream in anger and run forward to attack us all with their arms raised.

Just then, Grandpa steps in the way, and when they collide with him, he goes flying across the room and hits the wall hard.

"Grandpa!" I scream.

Locke laughs as I grab the two troll crosses, which brings the laughter to an immediate stop.

The Nurse

Darla

WHEN JON'S GRANDPA arrives, he has men with him who are in uniforms. I don't have to be told what to do. I run over to where they are standing. Then I look back. To my surprise, Jon is not behind me. He is standing between us and the *things* who held us captive, holding up the necklaces that the two of them were wearing moments ago and pointing at them as if they were some sort of weapon.

"Just come over here, Jon, where it is safe!" I yell. "You don't have to fight any more!"

Jon looks back over his shoulder. "This isn't over, Darla. Don't you understand? It will *never* be over!"

Locke and Dustin start to charge him as Jon says,

"May these troll crosses be inspired
As they grow to attack those that are expired.
May they burn and grow as I do tell
To send these evil spirits to the depths of Hel."

Then the things he is holding start to grow and flames engulf them as one goes screaming toward the man and the other goes straight for the boy's chest. In an instant, they both dissolve before my eyes. It's like an explosion but it's so bright, it blinds me.

After a few seconds, I look around in complete disbelief. "Um ... Where did they go?"

Jon turns to me. "They won't bother us any more, Darla. They were sent to the realm of Hel. Right where their kind belong!"

Overwhelmed, I feel myself go weak in the knees, and then a feeling of falling ... again.

WHEN I WAKE UP, I AM back in my tent and buried deep in my sleeping bag. *What? Was this all just a dream? A nightmare?* I look over at Jenny, who runs over to give me a hug.

"Darla, I was so scared! Don't ever run off like that again! You should know better than to go hiking on your own! Why would you do that? What were you thinking?"

I am now completely confused. "Wait! What are you talking about?"

"You have been missing since this morning, but Jon and Marc found you and brought you back here. You were tired and dehydrated, but I guess you just needed rest. You have been out quite a while now."

Just as I'm about to tell her that wasn't what happened, some of the men I saw earlier in uniforms come into the tent and ask Jenny to leave. Then one of them asks me, "Ms. Towns, are you okay?"

"No, I most certainly am not okay. I don't know what I am, but I am definitely not okay!"

"Miss, we just want to make sure you recover from that hike and that you never do that again. You gave us all quite a little scare."

The other one winks at me as if we have some sort of an inside secret, but I want no part of that and I don't get it because I know they were there, they saw it too!

"I don't know what you guys are talking about. As you good and well know, I was kidnapped and taken to some dark place underground where I saw a man turn into a cat. I saw *ghosts*. I saw Jon Bragg do things that I'm sure I'll never forget!"

They look at each other, and then one says, "I guess we're going to have to do it after all."

About then, a lady comes in, dressed as a nurse. "Hello, Darla. I am going to just talk to you for a bit. Is that okay?"

"Um ... No, I'd rather not talk to anyone alone right now. Nope. No way! Why don't you let Jenny back in here?"

"Sure, that's fine. Guys, bring the other girl back in here."

She then talks to Jenny. "Hello. Jenny, is it?"

Jenny nods.

"It's good to meet you, Jenny. It's really unfortunate that your friend, Darla here, went for a hike by herself. That was really scary, wasn't it?"

Jenny nods again.

"If Darla tells you anything else about today, you will ignore her because she is very tired and very shook up from getting lost and could say all kinds of wild things. Do you understand, Jenny?"

"Poor Darla, she is so confused."

"Yes, that's right. Darla is confused."

As I watch, Jenny looks over at me and shakes her head, as if she is so worried for me. Then Jenny tells me, "I'm so glad you're back, and I know you are confused. You can say whatever you need to say. It's okay."

Then the nurse turns to me and says, "Darla, look at me."

I try not to look, but I can't avoid her for some reason.

"Darla, I know you're confused and that you gave everyone a big scare. I also know you are very sorry for going hiking on your own and are grateful that you were found before anything terrible happened to you. You won't do anything like that again, will you, Darla?" I look at Jenny realizing what has happened and back to the nurse.

"I won't do anything like that again."

She nods at the officers, seemingly satisfied, and then they walk out of the tent.

As soon as they're gone, I ask Jenny, "That was weird, wasn't it?"

"What was weird?"

"The nurse who was just here."

"Oh," Jenny says. "She was really nice. I like her a lot! I'm sure you are just confused. You might say all kinds of things, but I'm sure you are just exhausted. It's okay, Darla. Just don't do anything like that ever again, okay?"

I shrug. This is going nowhere fast. "Okay, I guess."

"Promise me!" she yells.

"I promise."

Jenny smiles. "The guys are outside, waiting to talk to you."

Okay, sure.

I get outside and find Sam, Taylor, Marc, and Jon all standing there.

"How are you feeling? Better?" Marc asks.

"I feel fine. How are you, Marc?"

He laughs. Then everyone swallows me up in a group hug with each of them saying, "Don't do that again, Darla! Don't go off by yourself."

I step over to Jon. "You aren't going to tell me that I ran off on a hike, are you? That I'm just confused? We both know that isn't true."

He looks all around, in every direction, and then whispers, "Um, What are you talking about, Darla?"

"I remember everything, Jon."

He face turns all kinds of colors then quietly asks, "What do you remember?"

I glare at him. "Bragi, your secret is safe with me, scout's honor." I then give him a hug and whisper, "My hero."

The hug brings a bunch of snickers and sneers from the rest of the scouts. Whatever.

I am going to need some time to sort all of this out in my mind. It's a hot, jumbled mess right now, that much is a fact. I'm almost ninety percent sure that everything was real. Okay. I am almost seventy-five percent sure everything was real. Okay, I don't know what to think right now. Maybe it was a bit of dehydration and exhaustion; that would certainly be more believable.

Whether it happened or not, it's crystal clear that I am not supposed to talk about it. I decide that's a good thing. Nothing good can come from describing the impossible, and I would probably end up having to get my head examined. Actually, that might not be a terrible idea. Now *that* I could easily be convinced to do right now!

The Cleanup

Jon

THE NURSE AND THE APS visit everyone else that saw or heard anything, which is literally the entire camp, until they all fully believe that Darla went on a hike by herself and was brought back by Marc and me. She shouldn't be punished, or in any trouble. She just needs to not do it again. Everyone should be concerned for her, and if she says anything wild, we should all just ignore it as a part of the confusion from being lost, scared, and dehydrated.

I feel kind of bad about having to do this. Knowing the guys, she will *never* live this down, but there really isn't a better alternative. The world is simply not ready to hear about all things Asgardian.

Skipper is the last to go, and the nurse makes sure that she gives him instructions, as well, that include reinforcing "the buddy system next time." Skipper thinks that's a great idea and should avoid any future issues. He's really glad that nothing bad happened. But, to be on the safe side, the rest of the week should probably be canceled, and they should head back home. Of course, this really wasn't necessary since everyone thinks it was a minor incident. In order to do a full investigation, however, the APS needs the area cleared, they need to study everything while the evidence is as fresh as possible and that's just going to be too difficult to explain with the place crawling with people in uniforms.

Marc, Grandpa, and I, of course, all still know what really happened, and I guess so does Darla somehow.

Grandpa took a hard hit from Locke, so it's really good to see him up and somewhat walking around. I did the best I could to heal him while we were in the tunnels, but something interfered this time, or I guess I messed it up in some way. Maybe *I* was the confused one.

After we get done packing up, we all sit down to talk about how close of a scare that one was, and then Marc and I have some more questions for Grandpa.

"So, how can we be certain that Coach Locke and Dustin are indeed in Hel?"

Grandpa shrugs. "Honestly, we can't be certain. Hopefully, we'll never know because the only way we could is if we went there, and I know I have no intentions of doing that."

"Is there any way that a spirit can come back from Hel if that is where they went?" Marc asks.

"According to our beliefs, the answer is no. However, when it comes to what Loki is capable of, we really should be prepared for anything. The Loki line has shown some incredible resiliency throughout the years, from holding on to their powers to this latest ghost incident. One thing is for certain, Loki knows everything there is to know about Asgardians and the after-life realms. Plus, the goddess Hel, ruler of that realm, is indeed Loki's daughter."

That is not the most reassuring thing he could say. However, given what we know, both Marc and I understand what Grandpa is saying. It shouldn't be possible, but we should expect that if it is somehow possible, Loki will figure it out.

Before we get on the bus, Darla comes over to Marc and me. "I just wanted to thank both of you for coming to get me. No matter what, that was really brave and nice of you."

"Well, the whole troop really went out looking. Jon and I just happened to be the ones that found you," Marc says.

She looks at both of us then says, "Right ... Well, thank you." She gives us each a hug. "My heroes!" Then she asks, "Jon, can I talk to you alone, please?"

"Of course."

We take a short walk away from the buses, and she starts with, "I don't know if everything I saw was real or not right now, but I'm positive that at least some of it was. I'm also sure that the nurse was really hypnotizing everyone, or something like that. Look, I don't really need to know everything, but I expect you to be honest with me, got it?"

I nod and open my mouth to say something, but she continues, "Before you say anything that you are going to regret, just think about it, okay?"

"Okay."

"Scout's honor?" she asks.

I nod. "Scout's honor."

Then she finishes with, "I'll talk to you soon, Jon, or should I say *Bragi*?" She then winks and walks off over to the Blue Hill bus, and I am left wondering how it is possible that the nurse failed to alter her memory. Maybe some things are just too traumatic to be forgotten? Either way, there is no way I can say anything to anyone without them coming back and poking and prodding her to see why she remembers. I'm just going to have to let this one go, for her sake. Besides, I do trust her. She's all right.

On the way back on the bus, I try to decide if I should tell Marc or Grandpa about Darla remembering, but I'm not sure it's a good idea to put them in that position, especially since Grandpa has a responsibility to the APS. I could probably tell Marc, but then I would have to be worried about whether or not he might slip up and let it out on accident. There is no way he would do it on purpose, but accidents happen. Even to me.

No, it's better than I don't say anything to anyone, especially not before I know how much she really does remember. Maybe she just remembers a little bit of it, or maybe she remembers all of it. I need to know what I'm working with before I try to do anything about it.

I could also try to make her forget, but that would be sort of dishonest. I just got done telling her that I would be honest with her, and I feel resolved to keep that promise. She has been through enough.

If she does remember everything, I would rather that she didn't think she was having a breakdown or something. That would be incredibly insensitive of me, and that is just not something I could do to anyone, especially not to Darla.

Of all the things that could have happened and did happen on this scout outing, I don't know what was less likely—running into Dustin's and Coach Locke's ghosts or finding out that I like the mean girl from dance. I would have said both were impossible when this week started.

Hmm ... I like the mean girl from dance.

The Parents

Darla

AS SOON AS WE PULL into the school parking lot, all the parents come running up to see us. Well, except for my parents. My mother is standing by our car with her hands on her hips. I'm pretty sure she's ready to read me the riot act. Yep, great. This is exactly what I don't need right now after what I have been through.

As soon as I get over to the car, she just says, "Get in *now*!"

I wave at Jenny, who is with her parents, and then I get into the back seat.

Dad is in the front passenger seat, and Mother is driving. If she's in her car, she is driving, period. Dad couldn't care less, so this is quite normal for us.

Dad turns around and says, "Darlin', we were so worried about you. We heard that you wandered off on your own and got lost. Why would you do such a thing?"

I'm surprised that they already heard the news, but also not surprised. After all, we did come back a couple of days early, and that had to be explained somehow to our parents.

"That's not exactly what happened, Dad. It wasn't my fault."

Mother scoffs. "It sure sounds like it was your fault."

That attitude quickly shuts me down, and I quietly stare out the window the rest of the way home. As usual, she is not even going to try to listen to me, so there is really no point in even talking.

Once we pull into our driveway, I barely wait for the car to stop before I grab my bags and get out of the car. Then, before she can say anything, I tell her, "I am heading straight to my room, and I don't want to talk about it!"

Mother starts to protest, but Dad grabs her arm and shakes his head. She looks at him then says, "Fine, but this conversation is not over. Stay in your room until one of us comes to get you. Consider yourself grounded."

"Grounded? For how long?"

"Until I say you aren't."

"So, indefinitely then," I snap. "That's just great! Fine, whatever." I storm into the house, up the stairs, drop my bags, and jump face-first into my bed. Which, by the way, feels amazing after being in a sleeping bag and on a nasty dirt floor for several hours. In fact, this bed is divine.

In no time, I drift off into a nice, long nap. I'll stay here as long as I need to, too.

There was a point when I thought I would never see my room again, so I have no problem staying in here whatsoever. That is no punishment after what I have been through, which of course is something that nobody is going to believe.

I sleep soundly for a few hours, and I only know that because, when my dad comes into my room, it is already starting to get dark outside.

"Darlin', are you going to sleep through dinner?"

"Am I allowed to come out of my room to eat dinner?" I ask.

He chuckles. "Yes, darlin'. Come and get some dinner."

I grab his hand before he steps out the door and pull him down a little to give him a big hug. "I'm so glad to see you, Dad!"

He smiles. "I'm glad to see you, too, darlin'. Don't worry; all of this will blow over sooner than you think. I'm just glad you are home safe and sound."

"Dad, you have no idea how thankful I am to be home."

"Well, maybe that's what you should say to your mother. Let her know how grateful you are and how much you appreciate the dangers that exist out there now. The world can be a scary place."

"Yeah, tell me about it." I roll my eyes. "That much I know better than ever now. Thanks again, Dad."

"You're welcome, darlin', you're welcome."

As we are eating dinner, I decide to go with what Dad said and say to Mother, "I'm really grateful to be home, safe and sound. I learned a lot while I was camping. It's a lot more dangerous than I thought it could ever be."

Mother acknowledges that with a resolute, "You have to be smarter than that, especially when you are doing something that is already different. I know you like to push the boundaries Darla, but maybe you can just listen to me for once? Can't you just do dance, cheer, and all the other things that a proper girl should be doing?"

I nod. "Sure, Mother, I can do that. At least for a while."

She is a little surprised that there isn't an argument. In fact, she almost disagreed as a reflex before she says, "Good. It's settled. It's for the better, Darla. Trust me."

I'm not sure really if it is for the better or not but anything that gets me out of the doghouse is going to have to be good enough for now. We will cross the wrestling bridge when it comes, and it most definitely is still coming. I want to get better and better at *that* because, frankly, I don't ever want to feel the way I felt underground again. I don't want to be weak; I want to be strong. I want to be stronger than any boy so, if I need to defend myself, I have both the skills and the strength. Yep, I'm done with being the helpless victim. I want no part of that ever again!

Before dinner is done, she says, "I have some other happier news for you. Some of your cousins are coming from overseas to stay with us for a while. They are your age and are going through a lot, just like you. I'm hoping it will be easier if you all go through it together."

"Um ... Okay. What kinds of things exactly?"

"Oh, family things, dear. Like I said when we dropped you off for the scouting trip, we need to talk."

"Okay, then let's talk."

She looks at my dad. He knows the drill.

"That's my cue to head to the kitchen to do the dishes. You ladies have a nice chat." He gives me a wink as he heads out with the dirty dishes.

Mother starts by saying, "How much do you know about Norse mythology?"

"You have *got* to be kidding me! I know more now than I ever wanted to know!"

"Well, you're going to hear it again. Are you familiar with Ragnarök?"

"Yes," I tell her. "The gods and the giants fought, blah, blah, blah."

"Exactly," Mother says. "I want to talk about what went down there and about Aegir and Ran and, most importantly, their *nine* daughters."

Unbelievable! I thought I was done with *this*, but apparently, it's just beginning.

"Do I really *have* to, Mother?"

I get up to leave, but then she sternly says, "Darla Bara Towns, you sit down!"

Oh boy, I know it is bad when my middle name is used, so I take a seat in defeat.

DNA

Jon
Two Weeks Later...

IT'S TAKEN A COUPLE of weeks for the analysis to get back from all the tests that the APS ran after having us all leave Harmony Grove. They looked for any kind of magical footprint that could help them understand what happened, researching everything as thoroughly as possible from the camp, the graves, and the tunnels.

Marc and I have been waiting patiently for the results to come back, hoping that Grandpa will share the results with us. He hasn't heard anything, so none of us have access to them yet. Well, I should say *I* don't have access. Of course Marc doesn't since he is not an Asgardian.

While I am an Asgardian, I'm not really a part of the APS, other than having properly registered. I'm hopeful that will change over time, though. Grandpa is a member and, as far as I know, every Bragi in our family line has been with the APS since it was created. I wouldn't want to break that tradition. Plus, I completely believe in everything they are doing to make sure that all old-world powers stay in check and aren't abused.

I have continued reading up on the three after-life realms, just to see if I could find anything that we need to be worried about. Unfortunately for us, what I have found out is generally vague. There is clearly a belief, though, that it's possible for a spirit to cross realms and even to exist in multiple realms. However, that may or may not apply to Coach Locke and Dustin since they were specifically banned to Hel with an empowered troll cross. Unless they can find some other magical items in Hel, it is doubtful they will be granted access to any other realm. Of course, it's possible that one of the original gods could grant that access, but it's highly rare and unlikely, for a Loki, especially.

If the whole Loki line wasn't so renowned for being tricksters, they might have a better chance. I dare say that anyone who is tricked by a Loki is generally believed to get what is coming to them. It is becoming more and more rare as they lose more and more power and rights over all the realms.

Marc and I resumed our summer work to keep busy. While we were gone, Dad did our mowing for us so we didn't lose any clients. Of course he did a much better job, just like he told me on the phone, than we did, which isn't exactly helpful. I mean it was but now we have to hear about it over and over at least from the Wellington twins. I thanked Dad, but I also asked if, the next time he subs for us, if he could slack off a little so we don't have such big shoes to fill. His response was "A job isn't worth doing if you aren't going to do it right." So, that pretty much means he is not going to help us out with that request. I guess I can respect that. Well, I have to respect that, either way, because it is simply how it is. So, instead of asking him to slack off, I ask if he can go with us on our route to show us all the things he did that made our clients so happy. Happy clients are returning clients, and I'm sure we will try to do this again next year. After all, the Corolla isn't going to be making and paying for its own gas.

When Marc and I arrive home from mowing the Wellington house a second time, Grandpa is outside waiting for us. He still has a bit of a limp. Of course we told everyone that he fell while he was trying to help find the lost scout, which is sort of true. At least it's not a total lie. He's kind of a hero around town now and is well on his way to a full recovery.

As soon as we get the mower put away, he says, "Boys, we need to talk."

Yes!

We hurry downstairs for privacy and hopefully some good news, where Grandpa says, "The APS found the body of a man in the underground tunnels that is most likely the person that disturbed the grave by taking the troll cross. So, that explains how Locke was able to move about freely. They can't tell for sure, so if we get a chance Jon, we might use your gift if we can get access to the body to see what happened."

"Sure, Grandpa. When can we go?"

"Not so fast. Something else came up in their findings. They came across something they haven't seen in our area before. They found the DNA of a giant."

"Wait. Like a Ragnarök giant?" Marc asks.

"Yeah, but isn't Loki a giant?" I then ask.

"Very good, Jon. Yes, as a matter of fact, he is part giant and part god."

"Then, how can they be sure that the DNA found isn't from Locke?" I ask.

"Because they traced the line to a different giant family. Loki comes from Fárbauti, and this DNA was not from that line. We haven't seen it before, at least not in the United States."

"Okay ..." I drawl. "So, what does that mean?"

"It means that there may be giants around that we are not aware of, so we need to be on high alert."

"Again?" I whine. "Will we ever *not* be on high alert?"

Grandpa shrugs. "I don't know, Jon, but we are on high alert for now. Watch for any signs that anyone you run into is different. They might be very similar to an Asgardian, or they could seem completely normal but resistant to our ways."

"What does *resistant to our ways* mean?" I ask.

"They may not react to our magic like a human would. They most likely will be athletic and attractive. Giants have a way of taking a form that is appealing to humans and makes it a little easier for them to hide amongst them. Underneath that exterior, though, they could be quite hideous. It just depends on the giant."

"We understand, Grandpa," Marc says

"Good. If you see anything, or suspect anyone, you need to let me know, okay?"

Marc nods. "Okay."

I just nod to acknowledge that I understand, but my mind is racing. I almost immediately zero in on Sam because, well, he was giant in stature and pretty much good at everything. I also know that Darla was resistant to the nurse, but it can't be her, right? What if it is her? What am I going to do?

Summer Ends

Darla

WELL, IT HAS BEEN AN interesting couple of weeks. I'm not even sure what to say or do at this point, particularly after the news that my mother gave me. I decide that, for now at least, I am going to put that giant talk on the back burner. After all, we have a national dance competition before us, and I have a responsibility to our team.

We spend as much time as possible practicing each routine in excruciating detail to make sure that it's as close to perfect as possible. As Miss Sally says, "You only get one chance to win, so make it your best effort!" As if we were planning on just phoning it in and not giving it our all already. Whatever.

This entire team has been together for what seems like forever but, in reality, it is just since last fall. After all the practices and competitions, though, we are indeed a family of sorts. We even travel to Nationals together in caravans.

This year, Nationals are in Chicago, so it's not too far to drive. My family and Jess's family are driving together, since we have a duet and the exact same schedule.

The competition is intense here, as every company competing is exceptional, as they should be. Yet, all of us are ready. That includes Jill, even though she isn't dancing with us. Her family is here, too, which means Jon is here. I'm sure he is going to be watching our events, most likely to see Jess, but maybe now to support me, as well. I would like to think so, at least.

As Jess and I walk out on stage, I see Jon in the audience. It helps to inspire me to do my best, well even better than my best if that is possible.

Jess and I are in perfect sync, dancing as one unit. Every move is crisp and on point. Then, when we finish, we run backstage to see our family and friends. They all know that is the best we have ever done together, so we are excited to hear the results.

As a whole, we end up doing well in every dance. Miss Sally is so happy with us. We get to bring home all kinds of trophies for her to display at the school. I'm sure that will help recruit more dancers for next year.

Despite what I told my mother, I'm not sure if I want to try out next year or not. I might be done with dance for good. It's not going to get much better, and I still have wrestling on my mind. If I want to do that, I have a lot of training to do to get to the level I need to be to compete.

As Mother promised, eight of my cousins came to stay with us! Eight! I mean, the farmhouse is big enough, but that's kind of ridiculous, isn't it?

They are from Costa Rica, like my mother, and have similar attitudes to her, which is not going to be fun dealing with day in and day out, especially since we have to share a bathroom. Nine girls, one bathroom! Yeah, that's going to be fun. I do, however, also hope we get to share the chores. For right now, they are just getting settled in, but I'm hopeful that, once they do get "settled," they will have as much work to do around the house as I do. After all, that only seems fair.

They spend a lot of time talking with my mother. Actually, far more time than I spend talking to her. I'm sure they only talk about the whole Norse giant thing, but I'm still trying to stay as far away from *that* as possible. After what happened to me at camp, I have zero interest.

I didn't tell my mother about Jon or anything else I saw. As of right now, I don't know if she'll even believe me. And, if she does believe me, I'm not sure what she'll do. One thing is for certain; I need to talk to Jon. That's hard to do, though, when you're grounded. More specifically, when you don't have mobile phone privileges.

Every once in a while, when Mother steps out, Dad lets me have my phone for a few minutes. When he does now, I decide to see if Jon has an account with Snapchat. I want to be sure that nobody—namely my mother—with access to my phone can read the messages between us. Since chats disappear after they are read, it's perfect.

It turns out that he does have a Snapchat account. I find that out through Jill. Of course, she wanted to know why I wanted to bother talking to her "stupid brother." I get it. I don't have siblings, but with my cousins here, I am already thinking the same thing. *Who would want to speak to them?* They are not exactly friendly or fun to have a conversation with.

I send a chat to Jon, and now I just have to wait and see if he will reply.

It just says, "*Hey, John. It's Darla Towns. You can't tell by my handle, but it's me.*"

Jon types back, "*How do I know it's you, Darla?*"

I type back, "*Fireflies.*"

To which he types, "*Lightning bugs.*" He adds a smiley face to that then types, "*What's on your mind?*"

I type back to him, "*I have a giant problem over here at my house.*"

He replies, "*Tell me about it.*"

Don't miss out!

Visit the website below and you can sign up to receive emails whenever Kenney Myers publishes a new book. There's no charge and no obligation.

https://books2read.com/r/B-A-KKJN-IBQSB

BOOKS 2 READ

Connecting independent readers to independent writers.

Also by Kenney Myers

Jon Bragg

Jon Bragg Blue Essence

Jon Bragg Scout's Honor

Watch for more at https://www.kenneymyers.com.

About the Author

Kenney Myers is a husband and father of three children living and working in the Houston, TX area. He is originally from a small town in Iowa where he and his wife Jolene were high school sweethearts. You may be familiar with him as an actor in various films and TV shows or as a technology entrepreneur. He is best known for the TV show Kindly Kenney which is distributed worldwide by UKW Media.

Kenney enjoys writing fiction and creating worlds where characters develop and master special abilities. It's a great escape for him as a writer and is consistent with the types of books he loves to read.

Read more at https://www.kenneymyers.com.

CPSIA information can be obtained
at www.ICGtesting.com
Printed in the USA
LVHW021206271021
701683LV00005B/533

9 781736 571132